"I Owe You My Life," She Breathed.

"But you can't run my life for me, Sam."

He met her fiery gaze. "I'm collecting on that debt today," he said. "One day of your time doing what I'm asking of you in exchange for your life." His voice hardened. "That's my demand on you. And that's the way it'll be, Kelly."

Sam caught her arm as she tried to slap him. He couldn't be angry at her outburst. He would have felt the same. "Calm down," he growled. "You've got nothing to be angry about. I'm doing you a favor."

"You damn roughneck! Let me go! I'll show you! No one runs my life for me! You hear me, Sam Tyler! No one. Not even you!"

LINDSAY McKENNA

believes in living life to the fullest and has explored a wide variety of exciting and unusual careers. She began breaking mustangs at the age of fourteen, then went on to become a pilot in the Navy, a commercial artist and a fire fighter. She says her writing reflects "what I have learned about through life."

LINDSAY McKENNA
Texas Wildcat

Silhouette Desire

Originally Published by Silhouette Books
division of
Harlequin Enterprises Ltd.

First published in Great Britain 1985
by Mills & Boon Ltd, 15–16 Brook's Mews, London W1A 1DR

© Lindsay McKenna 1985

Silhouette, Silhouette Desire and Colophon are Trade Marks
of Harlequin Enterprises B.V.

ISBN 0 373 05003 8

22–0785

Made and printed in Great Britain by
Richard Clay (The Chaucer Press) Ltd,
Bungay, Suffolk

Other Silhouette Books by Lindsay McKenna

Silhouette Desire

Chase the Clouds
Wilderness Passion
Too Near the Fire

Silhouette Special Edition

Captive of Fate

*For further information about
Silhouette Books please write to:*

Jane Nicholls
Silhouette Books
PO Box 236
Thornton Road
Croydon
Surrey CR9 3RU

Dedicated to

Boots Hansen and Coots Matthews, blowout
specialists, who are genuine Texas heroes in the
finest sense—without you, your down home
country humor and generosity, this novel wouldn't
have been possible—thank you!
and
Alvin Moody, whose knowledge and friends
provided further insights into the Texas gas and oil
industry . . .
and
Jeanne Long, surely a Texan at heart, for her
friendship, creative ideas and enthusiasm, which
got this project off the ground and launched. One
hell of a lady and never a better friend—thank
you.

Texas
Wildcat

1

"All hell's broken loose, Kelly!"

Kelly tiredly raised her head. She stared blankly at Jake for a moment. Her officer manager's face was drawn. Her heart plummeted. What now? she wondered miserably. What else could go wrong? Brushing an auburn strand of hair away from her forehead, she sat up a little straighter in the huge leather chair.

"What's wrong?" Her voice sounded tired and strained after the events of the past week.

Jake grimaced, giving a sorrowful shake of his head. "Boots and Coots's office just called. Two of our monitor pipes blew up on them."

"Oh, no!" Kelly groaned, slumping back into the chair. "How? I mean . . ."

Jake came inside the door and shut it softly behind him. "They're sending Sam Tyler over to tell us about it."

She frowned, pushing aside the mountain of paper-work. "Who's he?"

"Number three man in the outfit, that's who. They're angry, Kelly. We're gonna lose the account."

Kelly made an agitated gesture, then got to her feet. "Dad never made bad pipe. What's going on, Jake? I don't understand it," she muttered, walking around the large square desk. She fought back tears of remembrance. Tears of grief. Only a week ago her father, a Texas wildcatter as well as the president of Blanchard Pipe, had been sitting in this office. Now, he was dead. Dead because of a senseless automobile accident. A drunk driver had ended the life of the person she loved more than anyone in the world. Kelly's green eyes narrowed with pain as she stared over at Jake. She chastised herself for not knowing more of her father's business. Now, it was up to her to run the multimillion-dollar company, which made a variety of pipe for the oil and gas industry around the world.

Placing a slender hand on her brow, she massaged her temples. She had to think coherently regardless of the circumstances. Boots and Coots were one of their major buyers. They used Blanchard pipe at oil and gas well blowouts to spray water on the raging inferno while their men worked to put the fire out.

"Who spoke to you, Jake?" she asked, her voice barely above a whisper.

"Boots Hansen did."

"What happened?"

Jake released a heavy sigh. "Coots Matthews and Sam Tyler were up on a call in Canada. They trucked in a load of our pipe for the job. Their men had set up the unmanned water monitors close to the gas fire to protect the crew working beneath it. When Sam went in to help with the welding on the blowout preventer our pipe failed on two out of the six water monitors." Jake shook his head, stealing a glance over at Kelly. "That type of fire can reach temperatures of twenty-two hundred degrees Fahrenheit. A heavy water fog pattern is used so the men can work at the mouth of the well."

Kelly's full lips thinned. "Don't tell me they were injured?"

"'Fraid so, Kelly. They put Slim Hudson in a burn unit up in Canada. Tyler was burned too, but apparently not as badly. The team just landed at the airport and he's on his way over here right now."

It was far more serious than she had first thought. Blanchard pipe was designed to withstand thousands of pounds of water pressure hurtling through it for months on end without failure. This was the third time within a month that their pipe had buckled during a critical phase. Word was getting around. The business her father had started twenty years ago was in danger of failing because of it.

Tears glittered in Kelly's green eyes as she lifted her chin. "Okay, Jake, bring Mr. Tyler to me when he gets here. I want to deal with this one personally. Boots and Coots have been good customers for too long. This *has* to be investigated."

"Man, you're telling me. I feel bad about this one."

"Is Slim going to be all right?"

Jake managed a sliver of a smile. "You know Texans, Kelly. We're all tougher than horseshoe nails. Yeah, he'll make it."

"Have Susan get more information. I want to know when they'll transfer Slim back to Houston," Kelly ordered.

Walking dejectedly back to the leather chair, Kelly stared at the floor. Normally, her shoulders were straight and proud. Today they slumped. The guilt bore down on her. Why hadn't she gotten more involved in her father's business this last year before his death? The answer was simple: her crumbling marriage had finally fallen apart. This past year she had been picking up the bits and pieces of her psyche and she had thought it best not to return to the business world full time until she had her life under control.

Todd, her ex-husband, had always opposed her working. He wanted no wife of his to be a corporate executive. Kelly had relinquished her position as vice-president when she left Houston to marry, but she had insisted on helping her father as a regional director. Her involvement with the business had led to one horrible argument after another. After five years of quarrels, Kelly had given up on the faltering marriage, unwilling to suffocate beneath Todd's restrictions. But she was still suffering from the effects of the divorce.

Before she had time to consider all those effects, the door of her office was jerked open. Kelly's eyes widened as she met the angry blue gaze directed at her. She froze, fingers resting on the desk, facing her adversary. He wore the white coveralls that were synonymous with Boots and Coots Company. Over the left pocket was the name, Sam, in blue embroidery. Kelly's heart leaped. He wasn't a huge man, but the animal power within him took her breath away. She had never met him before, yet her senses were instantly affected by him. His blue eyes narrowed on her. The face, darkly tanned by the Texas sun, was square, the jaw uncompromising. His black hair was neatly trimmed and hidden beneath a white baseball cap with the Boots and Coots symbol upon it. Involuntarily, Kelly took a step back, her legs brushing against the chair. If it weren't for his mouth, she would have been completely intimidated by him. But it was a kind mouth, though it was drawn now into a thin line.

"I'm Sam Tyler. Where's Blanchard?" he ground out. Sam Tyler was feeling irritated with the fact that his right arm had to remain in a sling for the next week. He glared at the woman in front of him. "We've got a score to settle with him." He halted at the desk and unceremoniously dropped a piece of aluminum pipe on it. "Blanchard integrity!" he snarled. "Take a look, honey. The old man's company can go to hell for this," he continued, jabbing his square index finger down at the pipe. One end was blown completely apart, its normally smooth exterior now jagged, razor sharp splinters.

The smarting pain of the burns on his shoulder and upper arm fueled Sam's anger. The woman standing before him appeared as tired as he felt. Her eyes were the color of dark emeralds. Was she Blanchard's secretary? Despite the pallor of her face and the darkness beneath her large eyes, she was damn good looking. Sam squelched those thoughts. "Where is the old—"

"Dead."

Sam's eyes widened. "What are you talking about? I just talked to him two weeks ago."

Kelly's hands clenched into fists at her sides. "I said he's dead. Does that compute? He was killed last week in an automobile accident."

Sam swallowed his anger. A frown formed on his

forehead and he reached up, taking off the cap. "I'm sorry," he muttered. "Then who are you? His secretary?"

"I'm his daughter, Mr. Tyler. Look," she began, in a strained voice, "sit down. I'll have Susan bring us some coffee. I just heard about the pipe blowing. I need more information."

Sam's mouth softened and he took a step back. "Yeah," he agreed, his voice losing its hard edge. "I guess we could both use a cup of coffee."

Kelly tried to still her racing heart. This man was a stranger to her, so why was she responding to him so strongly? I must be closer to exhaustion than I thought. She had to get some sleep soon or . . . Kelly brushed her thoughts aside and called Susan to bring coffee. Sam had seated himself in the chair before her desk. Her gaze settled on his heavily bandaged left arm and the sling.

"I'm sorry," she murmured. "Jake told me you and Slim got burned." She regarded him gravely. "It shouldn't have happened."

Running his strong looking fingers through his dark hair, Sam held her gaze. In that instant she looked so damned fragile; a china doll that had been fractured. The anger he had carried all the way home on the plane dissipated. He judged her height around five feet nine. Thick, auburn hair tumbled in graceful abandon around her shoulders, barely brushing her breasts. The simple black dress with its white collar and french cuffs increased her look of vulnerability. Her complexion appeared washed out. Sam's eyes narrowed as he continued to study her. Why hadn't he seen her around Houston? Where had Blanchard been hiding his daughter? She appeared to be almost ethereal. At that moment he wanted to reach out and touch her to see if she was real. Would she disappear like a cloud on a scorching Texas day?

"I shouldn't have come barging in here like a steam roller, either," he apologized. "It's just that we're all pretty upset by Slim's injury."

Susan entered, interrupting the tense conversation. With their respective cups of coffee in hand, they waited until the secretary left the office. Kelly walked over to the desk and sat down. "You had every right to be angry, Mr. . . ."

"Call me Sam," he insisted.

It would be easy to call him by his first name. The sudden warmth in his voice eased the tension between them. "Let's discuss your problem with the pipe," she suggested, pulling over a notebook and a pencil. "Can you tell me what led up to the pipe's failure?"

Sam hesitated, sensing her utter exhaustion. "Look," he began on a more conciliatory note, "you don't need this right on top of your father's death. I could speak to Jake. We've dealt with him quite a bit in the past."

Kelly shook her head. "No," she returned, a smile pulling at one corner of her mouth, "I need to be kept busy right now." The smile disappeared as she stared over at the pipe. "And this incident has top priority." She was thankful her father wasn't here to witness this. His pride in producing a quality product was well known; this would have broken his heart.

Sam leaned forward, resting his one elbow on his long thigh. "You're taking over his business, then?"

"Yes."

Sam nodded. She had guts. He liked the fire he saw flickering in the depths of her wide, transparent eyes.

17

"Okay," he agreed, "let me fill you in on the details of the pipe blowing, then."

"Fine. Start at the top, Sam."

He leaned back, feeling the dull pain from the second-degree burns across his right shoulder and upper arm. He disdained pain killers because he didn't want the loss of alertness they caused. "We got a call to cap a Canadian gas well up in the province of Alberta. Coots was available and the three of us flew up."

"And the pipe?"

"Trucked in. It took Pete four days to make the drive."

Kelly nodded. It was August and it must have been warm even up in Canada at the time. "Do you remember the temperature on the day our pipe failed?"

He shrugged one broad shoulder. A shoulder that looked as though it could carry the weight of the world on it. Kelly found herself wishing she could simply lay her head on it for just a moment . . . to find a moment's peace. Her rambling thoughts surprised her. Sam Tyler was a complete stranger to her! Wearily, she touched her brow, confused by her own chaotic emotional reaction.

"It was eighty-two degrees Fahrenheit, but near the blowout it was close to twenty-five hundred degrees. We worked under a galvanized roof while welding the blowout preventer to the pipe. With the shielding of the roof plus the water fog, it was a livable two hundred degrees underneath."

"Were you aware of a front coming through? What was the weather situation at the time?"

He gave her an intent look. "What are you getting at? You think high temperature and high barometric pressure might have had something to do with the pipe failing?"

Kelly felt her stomach tighten. "I don't know. All I want are the facts. We'll have our lab analyze this pipe. The lab people will have to have all available data in order to make a correct analysis." Her voice sounded just as clipped as his. But she didn't want to fight. She wanted peace. She wanted to be held by strong, protecting arms. And there had been no one for the last year of her life. No one who would allow her to lean on him for a moment to try to gather her emotional strength.

"I'll also need to know how many thousands of pounds of pressure were being pumped through the pipe."

"I don't remember right offhand. Pete was our pressure specialist on that job. A full report is logged in on every blowout we cap. It might be better if you come over to the office at Port Neches tomorrow and read through it. Coots will be finishing it tonight."

Kelly allowed the pencil to slip from her fingers. She gazed across the room at Sam Tyler. She didn't blame him for his anger over their injuries. "When will they be flying Slim back here to Houston?"

Surprise flared briefly in his eyes. "Why?"

"Because, Mr. Tyler, I want to see him and personally apologize. Here at my father's company we're used to keeping oil men safe, not maiming them." Her voice broke and Kelly felt the tears rush into her eyes, blurring her vision. She got up and turned, walking resolutely to the window. Her jaw was clenched and rigid as she fought back the deluge that threatened to overwhelm her. She heard Sam get up, heard the soft brush of his boots against the carpet.

"I'll be over at Boots and Coots tomorrow morning at

nine A.M., Mr. Tyler,'' she forced out in a brusque manner to hide her tears. Drawing her shoulders up, she silently willed him not to touch her.

Sam halted a few feet from where she stood. Her clean profile was silhouetted against the bright blue of the Texas sky. It was a face filled with stubbornness and pride. But he also saw sensitivity and gentleness there. Her lower lip trembled, and Sam sensed that she was very close to tears. His natural reaction was to reach out and comfort her. But the angle of her tense body warned him off. Dropping his gaze, he said, ''Okay, we'll see you tomorrow morning, Ms. Blanchard. And I'm sorry about your father's death. . . .''

Kelly waited until she heard the door close before burying her face in her hands. She took several deep, ragged breaths, controlling her anguish. The sudden tenderness and concern that Sam Tyler had displayed had nearly broken her in two. She had had a wild urge to turn and throw herself into his arms. Instinctively, she knew that he would have allowed her to cry freely without demanding an explanation. Groaning softly, Kelly walked back to the desk. Opening the drawer on the right, she grabbed a handkerchief and blotted her eyes.

The buzzer rang and Kelly picked up the phone.

''Yes, Susan?''

There was hesitation in the secretary's voice. ''Ms. Blanchard, a Mr. Gage Wallace of Wallace Steel is here to see you.''

Kelly stood frozen. No! Not now! And not him! Pursing her lips, she said, ''Tell him I'm busy, Susan. He made no appointment and I don't feel up to seeing anyone else today. Whether he likes it or not, he has to make an appointment like everyone else.''

She hadn't meant to slam the phone down, but she did anyway.

The door to her office opened moments later and Kelly looked up from behind the desk. Gage Wallace slipped in, quietly shutting the door.

"I've come to extend my condolences, Kelly.''

A surge of emotion rose in her. It took the last of her efforts to remain calm. At age forty-two Wallace was a slender man with prematurely graying hair. Like most image-conscious businessmen, he was impeccably dressed in a dark, pinstripe suit. His brown eyes were narrowed upon her face. "Forgive an old friend for disregarding your secretary's orders.'' He walked up to the desk and handed her a bouquet of tiger lilies, pink tea roses and purple iris.

Kelly stared at the flowers. Her emerald eyes darkened. "You're a little late with funeral flowers, Gage.''

A slight smile drifted across his lean face. "These are for you, Kelly. I thought they might brighten up your day.''

Her glare was frosty and laden with contempt as she rose from her chair. "The only thing that will brighten up my day is for you to get out of here!''

Gage casually dropped the bouquet on the desk. He seemed completely undisturbed by her outburst. It was as if he were waiting for a child to tire of her temper tantrum. "I was out of the country at the time of your father's death. Otherwise, I would have attended the funeral and given you moral support.''

Her nostrils flared. "Take your lies somewhere else,

Gage! You never cared for anyone longer than it took you to take their money!'' Kelly choked back a sob. Oh, God, she couldn't cry! Not in front of this man who had been like an evil shadow in her father's life and her own.

"Look," he continued smoothly, "I know you're terribly upset by what happened. It's all over the industry that Blanchard pipe has failed on several blowouts." He gave a practiced smile that was supposed to win her over. "Sure I can't interest you in using Wallace Steel Mills? I can assure you our formulas are up to the best standards. Why not switch? Now would be a perfect time. You can't afford to buy any more pipe from R and B Steel. It will ruin your company's reputation if another pipe blows under stress. You could lose the whole business, Kelly."

She was trembling. In an effort to hide her distress, she leaned forward in an aggressive stance. "We have nothing to discuss, Gage. Not a damn thing. It's typical of you to take advantage of a traumatic human event and try to make a buck out of it. You figure if I'm grief-stricken, I'll just fall for your plan." Her eyes sparked with disgust. "I may be upset but that doesn't interfere with my business sense! Now get out!" She marched to the door and jerked it open.

He watched her for several seconds. "I'll call on you sometime early next week. We'll have dinner—"

"You don't run my life, Gage. You never did. Just because you and Todd were partners once, that doesn't give you access to me. I watched you run my ex-husband out of the business. I know your kind even if he didn't." Her voice shook. "Next time, you make an appointment. This is the last time you take advantage of me, my father's business or anything having to do with us."

Gage gave her a chilling smile as he hesitated at the

door. "Someday, Kelly," he began softly, "some man will break that fiery spirit of yours and put you in your rightful place. You're one hell of a strong-willed woman. You need a strong man. Todd was too weak for you."

Kelly smiled grimly. "And you can take your opinions with you, too. The man I love won't want to 'break me,' as you put it, Gage. But then, that's all you know: smash and destroy."

Gage smiled steadily, his eyes opaque. "You know, there are some parts of your spirit I like."

"Get out."

"I'll call on you next week."

"Don't bother."

2

─❊❊❊❊❊❊❊❊❊❊─

S am!" Boots Hansen thundered. Unable to sit still longer than two minutes at any given time, Boots got up from behind the desk in his spacious office. Like all his employees, he wore white coveralls. Just as he came around the desk, Sam appeared at the door. "There you are. Come on in. You finally get cleaned up?"

Sam nodded. After leaving the office of Blanchard Pipe, he had gone home to shower, shave and change clothes. Trying to shave with his left hand had proved disastrous. Right-handed by nature, Sam had nicked himself more than once.

Boots's blue eyes twinkled. "What the hell happened to you, boy?" A wide grin spread across his full face. "Remind me not to let you use a razor anymore."

Sam took the teasing in stride. He touched his jaw where one of several cuts had occurred. "I'm tempted to rip this sling off my arm and say to hell with it. I don't think I can wait a week to get this damn thing off,'' he growled. Making himself comfortable in one of the leather chairs, he waited for Boots to sit down.

"You up to playing messenger boy? Or do you want to rest? You look kinda peaked.''

Sam grinned. He had been with the oil firefighting company for three years. His employers' homespun sense of humor and genuine concern were their trademarks in the industry. No one would make an outward fuss over Sam's burn injuries. But the concern lingering in Boots's blue eyes told Sam that he was more than a little worried. "No, I'm fine," he lied. His shoulder hurt like hell.

With a decisive nod of his head, Boots pushed a set of papers toward Sam. "Good. Coots just finished up with the report on Well Number 561. Kelly Blanchard called and said she wanted to read that report as soon as possible. You mind driving by the Royden Oaks section and dropping this off to her on your way home?"

Sam reached over for the report. "Royden Oaks, huh? That's the richest part of Houston."

"Yeah. Guess the little gal flew down from Pittsburgh when her father died. She's staying at his house.'' Boots pushed his thinning blond hair off his broad forehead. "What'd she have to say about the pipe failing?"

Sam wanted to convey her genuine apology. He had silently applauded her courage. There were few women he knew who could handle the death of a loved one and then go to work to keep a multimillion-dollar company afloat. "She's concerned, Boots. And she wants to get to the bottom of the problem."

Boots gave a sigh. "We can't have it happen again, Sam. We're gonna have to go somewhere else to buy pipe. I already have five different pipe companies crying to come over and sell us their wares. I feel bad about this. Blanchard was a good-hearted guy and we've bought their pipe for years. Damn," he said, rising. "It doesn't make sense, Sam. That pipe's withstood the Canadian winters at sixty below and been tested in the Persian Gulf where it's a hundred and fifteen degrees in the damn shade." He scratched his head. "Coots and I are going to have a meeting with her tomorrow morning and give her the bad news." He shook his head in a mournful gesture. "Get going, son, you're looking like hell. What you need is two days' worth of sleep. Tomorrow's Friday, so don't bother coming in. We'll see you Monday unless we're called in on something big."

Sam rose. "Okay, I'll see you Monday."

The sun was dipping closer to the western horizon as he drove down the freeway toward the Royden Oaks section of Houston. Sam never tired of the Houston skyline which rose dramatically into the vivid blue Texas sky. Many of the buildings were covered with reflective glass, giving the city a magical quality. It was a city of mirrors. His thoughts switched to Kelly Blanchard. One look at her exhausted features had made him wince inwardly. He felt guilty about barging in and lashing out at her in anger. But he had acted out of frustration over Slim getting injured. Before reaching the Royden Oaks area, he stopped at a florist shop and bought flowers.

Kelly had just finished a hot bath and slipped into a floor-length muslin robe of pale pink when the doorbell sounded. The bell rang hollowly through the depths of the large, silent house. She had taken the guest bedroom on the first floor, not wanting to sleep upstairs in her father's bedroom. Padding barefooted down the long, tiled hall, Kelly opened the door. Her eyes widened in surprise as she saw Sam Tyler standing there with a bouquet of delicate violets in his large hand. He smiled at her hesitantly.

"Here," he said, giving them to her, "these are for you. A peace offering for the way I behaved earlier. And here's that report you asked to see. There are a couple of things Coots wanted me to point out to you before I left."

Her lips parted as she took the lovely violets and the report. "Thank you," she whispered, inhaling the fragrance of the flowers. "Please, come in. You look awfully tired."

Sam managed a smile. "You, on the other hand, look better than when I first met you."

Kelly returned his warm smile, her depressed spirits suddenly buoyed by his presence. "A bath can do wonders, believe me." She smelled the flowers one more time after shutting the door. The memory of Wallace's bouquet came back sharply. With Wallace, there was always an angle, an ulterior motive for everything he did. Looking at Sam Tyler's broad shoulders and massive back as he walked in front of her, she couldn't imagine him being like that.

"Come to the study, Sam," she invited. "I'm afraid I'm still learning the layout of Dad's house. He bought it after I left Houston, you see. I get lost in it when I'm not concentrating on where I'm going."

Sam gazed appreciatively around the study. It was a huge library filled with leather-bound books, Oriental rugs and expensive antique furniture. He settled on the couch. "It's quite a place," he agreed. "Will you be staying here from now on?" It was a thoroughly personal question and one that he probably shouldn't have asked. Sam noted she wore no wedding ring on her left hand. She turned to him, lifting her shoulders. "I don't honestly know yet. Would you like a drink?"

"Yes."

"How about some whiskey?"

He watched as she walked to the liquor cabinet. There was a wonderful gazellelike grace to her walk. He would never tire of watching her. Her dark auburn hair lay thickly on her shoulders, the red highlights glinting like molten fire. "Why whiskey?"

"You looked as though you could handle it," Kelly remarked.

"Oh?"

"You're the rugged outdoors type of man." She gave him a shy look, as if she realized her remark was too personal for the circumstances. "You look as if you could handle anything or anyone."

Sam stood and walked over to her. He reached out and took the tumbler from her. Their fingers met for only an instant but he was aware of a pleasant sensation as he touched her flesh. "I damn near blew up at you today," he murmured, "and I apologize. That's what the flowers are for. Boots told me you flew in as soon as your father died and began running his company." He lifted his glass in salute to her as she sat down near him on the couch. "Here's to a lady with courage when it counts."

Kelly felt heat racing up from her neck into her face. She took a sip of wine, wishing she could steady the sudden pounding of her heart. Tears welled in her eyes as she stared over at Sam. He was being so kind, and she'd gone through so much this week.

"I'm sorry," she mumbled. But the tears came anyway and she put the drink down on the coffee table. Her insides were quaking and she wanted to release the backlog of grief she had held in abeyance since the funeral. Her vision blurred as she sat there with both hands against her cheeks. Her lashes were thick with tears. Embarrassed, Kelly rose. "I . . . I . . . can't talk just now. . . ."

He was on his feet in one fluid motion, a huge cat uncoiling from his resting position. Kelly felt the natural warmth of his body as he placed his good arm around her shoulders, drawing her close. His work-roughened hand slid across the muslin, creating a tingling sensation in her flesh. The tender look on his face only increased her need to be held. A small cry escaped from her as she buried her face against his barrellike chest.

"It's all right," Sam whispered against her ear. "I'll just hold you, honey. Go ahead and cry." She was warm, curving perfectly against the more angular planes of his body. Sam inhaled the fresh, sweet fragrance of her silken hair as he rested his jaw lightly against her head. He felt her body shake with sobs and his grip tightened around her. He wished he had use of his right arm so he could cradle her protectively in his embrace.

The textured weave of the coveralls pressed against Kelly's cheek as she leaned her head on his chest. His gentle voice encouraged her to vent the grief. He was a stranger. And yet, her heart opened to him like a flower to the rays of the sun. There were no recriminations from Sam Tyler for her unexpected tears. Somehow, Kelly sensed Sam would take this in stride without being embarrassed. Finally, the tears lessened. She remained against him, aware, for the first time, of the drumbeat of his heart. It was a soothing sound and Kelly shut her eyes tightly, needing the strength he was giving her.

"Better?" he inquired in a hushed tone, his mouth against her hair.

She gave a convulsive nod of her head, wanting, needing his arm around her body for just one more moment. She felt his fingers tighten momentarily on her shoulder, and unconsciously she nuzzled against his chest.

"Come on," he urged, "let's sit down."

She sniffed. Lifting her eyes, she met Sam's eyes. His blue gaze held a tender light in its depth. "I'm sorry," she mumbled, "I don't normally go around crying. . . ."

A slight smile lifted one corner of his sensual mouth. "You don't strike me as the kind of woman who goes around crying on anyone's shoulder. So I consider it quite a compliment."

Her shoulders drooped as she sat down next to him. Kelly buried her face in her hands for a moment. She was grateful for their closeness. "You've been through your own personal hell," she whispered, "I shouldn't be laying my troubles at your doorstep."

Sam shook his head, reached out and slid his arm around her shoulders. "No you don't," he admonished gently. "Your father had one hell of a reputation as a fighter. And you're his daughter. I'd wager you get just as stiff-necked and proud as he was. You don't let anyone help you."

Kelly responded to his touch. It was all so crazy. Sam Tyler was a stranger. He had come over to drop off the report. Nothing more. But here she was, leaning against his warm strong body, weeping without restraint. She closed her eyes, needing the solace he provided. Her world had gone berserk and she was far too exhausted to try to halt the cataclysmic events tearing her life apart. Sam Tyler represented the only available source of stability at the moment.

"You're right," she returned, her voice nearly inaudible. She took a deep breath and tried to compose herself as he continued to lightly massage her shoulders. "I am my father's daughter."

Sam managed a soft snort. "Proud, Irish and Texan. One hell of a belligerent combination," he said without rancor. He gazed down at her with newfound tenderness. It would be easy to close the inches separating them and kiss her. He longed to feel the pliancy of her lips beneath his mouth . . . what the hell was he thinking about? Sam jerked his torrid thoughts up short.

"Just rest, honey," he urged quietly. "I'll sit here and hold you for as long as you need." He watched as her drooping lids closed. Dark lashes swept across her translucent skin like auburn crescents. The rise and fall of her breasts against him lessened. As the minutes passed her breathing became shallow, indicating that she had fallen asleep. An odd smile curved Sam's mouth. His day was certainly turning out to hold one surprise after another.

He hadn't expected to find a woman in charge of Blanchard when he went charging in there with the blown section of pipe. He hadn't expected to meet a woman who had beauty, intelligence and genuine compassion. Sam looked back down at her. Yes, that was what appealed to him the most about her: the fact that she really cared. Old man Blanchard had always wanted to satisfy his customers by providing a quality product.

And his lovely, headstrong daughter was cast from the same mold. Sam found her appealing and couldn't regret the explosive meeting that had brought them together.

He drew in a breath and his broad brow furrowed with worry. You'd better sleep, Kelly Blanchard, he thought to himself, because when you wake up, there will be more problems to deal with. His frown deepened. How could this tall, proud woman affect him so deeply? Was it her spitfire quality? Her courage? Grimacing, Sam knew he had no easy answer. All he was sure of was that when the situation calmed down, he wanted the opportunity to know her better.

There were a myriad of questions he wanted to ask. Did she have someone waiting for her back in Pittsburgh? More than likely. She was too damn pretty not to have a crowd of male admirers around her at all times. Children? If he recalled correctly, he remembered that Blanchard's only daughter had gotten a divorce a year ago. And it had been a messy one according to the gossip around the oil and gas industry. In this industry, everyone knew everyone else's business. Had her ex-husband been unable to deal with her? Sam's blue eyes twinkled at that thought. Yes, she would be a handful for any man who was threatened by a competent, assertive young woman with brains and moxie to back her up.

He remained an hour before carefully extricating himself and gently depositing Kelly on the couch. He located an afghan and placed it over her. Dusk was settling over the city and if he didn't leave now, he'd end up falling asleep with her cradled in the crook of his good arm. That wasn't a bad thought. But he sensed she would feel embarrassed enough about her outburst of tears. Proud women cried in private. A lambent flame burned in his eyes as he reached down, allowing his fingers to trail through the thick tresses of her hair. He had been right: it was like silk. Reluctantly, he broke contact and left the report on the desk with several scribbled notes pointing out certain paragraphs of the text that needed her attention.

"I'm sorry, Kelly, we just can't use Blanchard Pipe anymore." Coots Matthews gave her a regretful look, casting an uneasy glance at his partner, Boots Hansen. "We'd like to, honey, but this is the third time in a month that pipe has failed. We can't risk our men this way. Conditions at an oil or gas blowout are hazardous enough without our being unable to trust our water piping." Coots shifted uncomfortably. "You understand?"

Kelly remained silent as she listened to their softly spoken apology. When she had groggily awakened around midnight the night before a flood of embarrassment had filled her. But after reading the report well into the early morning hours, she had more serious things to worry about than her behavior with Sam Tyler. She was convinced something was terribly wrong at Blanchard Pipe.

Her green eyes flashed with pent-up annoyance. "Boots, how long did you know my Dad?"

"A good twenty years," he admitted.

Kelly swung her gaze to Coots. He was the taller and quieter of the famous firefighting duo. Today his face was even more serious than usual. "How about you, Coots?"

"I recollect it was going on twenty-five."

She straightened up in the chair. They sat in the conference room at an oval mahogany table. She tapped her finger on the wood surface. "And never once in all those years did you see a Blanchard pipe blow?" Her voice was charged with emotion and conviction. She knew her father's standards of excellence in a product. He believed in paying a good price for good quality material. "Well?" she demanded, her voice becoming husky.

Coots exchanged a mournful look with his partner. "No, honey, none of it ever failed us."

Her nostrils flared and she threw back her shoulders. "Listen, I read that report. And there wasn't enough evidence in it. I'm not willing to concede that it was completely our fault." She looked each man in the eye. It was a risky ploy and her stomach was knotting in terror over their possible reactions.

Coots frowned, scratching his head. "Now wait a minute—"

Kelly was on her feet. "No, you wait. I want another chance from both of you. For my Dad, if nothing else. I'll be damned if I'm going to allow three pipe failures to ruin his business and reputation!" Her voice became strained with unshed tears. "Dad never cheated anyone in his whole life! Don't you see? He'd never cheat on specifications for metal on these pipes. I've got to know what went wrong. Something had to induce the metal failure."

Boots and Coots exchanged glances. She unconsciously held her breath, watching their facial expressions. "Look," she went on, heedless of what they might think, "I have a plan. On your next blowout call, take me along. Me and a Blanchard pipe. I'll pay to bring other pipe along from another manufacturer of your choice just in case ours does fail. I want—no, need—to go out in the field with you guys and see why our pipe failed. At least let me do this before you decide."

Boots puckered up his mouth and expelled a long breath of air. "I don't have a problem with that, Kelly. But hell, we can get called anywhere in the world."

"Besides that," Coots rumbled in his baritone, "you know these fires may last up to six months before they're put out." He glanced up at her with his dark brown eyes. "You got that kind of time to spend out at a site, Kelly?"

She placed her hands on her hips. "For the sake of the men whose lives depend on Blanchard Pipe, I'll make the time. I simply want to be on site for a couple of weeks to record temperature, barometric pressure and other variable factors that might have overstressed our product. I have to see it for myself." In reality, Kelly knew that she could have sent someone else from the company, but it was her willingness to become personally involved that would convince Boots and Coots to give her pipe a second chance. "In the meantime, I've got our lab people and an independent metallurgical lab analyzing the pipe that failed. I'll have the results in two weeks. If our design or R and B Steel did not comply with our specs, I'll be the first to tell you." Her green eyes darkened to a jade color. "We've never sold bad pipe to anyone in the world and I won't start now."

Coots raised his eyebrows, his long face clearly revealing his surprise. "We never did think your Dad cheated us, Kelly. Hell, we've done business with him for a long time. I'm just worried about our men getting injured again."

"I know that," she went on. "And Blanchard will pick up Slim and Sam's medical expenses. It's the least we can do. My company's reputation is on the line. I can't afford one more failure or twenty years of my Dad's efforts will go down a dry hole."

Boots allowed a partial grin. "You sure as hell are your father's daughter." He exchanged a glance with Coots. "Sam was say'n the same thing this morning. He felt we ought to give you another chance. He's highly respected in our field. Sam's speciality is fluid hydraulics and particularly water systems. So we kinda took his opinion on this problem with a great deal of seriousness."

Kelly swallowed her surprise. "He did?"

"Sure did, honey," Boots spoke up, getting quickly to his feet. He jammed the white baseball cap back on his head. "Okay, it's settled. You'll go with us on the next call. We'll need another load of pipe—"

"It's on its way over here right now," Kelly interrupted, smiling for the first time.

Coots grinned and gave her a wink. "Okay, Kelly Blanchard, we got a deal." He thrust his hand across the table, gripping her hand.

Kelly nodded. "You bet you do. And believe me, neither of you will regret your decision."

Boot's smile widened. "Listen, I'm partial to red-headed Texas tornados. Like your father's, your word's good enough for us, Kelly." He pointed his finger at her. "Have our secretary, Arlene, outfit you with our coveralls before you leave here today."

Kelly's eyebrows rose. "Why?"

"If you're going out on a job with us, you'd better wear our uniform. Otherwise, the police or military are apt to haul you off the site. We'll have Arlene make up a badge for you, too. In the meanwhile, pack one suitcase with bare essentials and be ready to move on a moment's notice."

Coots's rolling laugh filled the room. "You know what he means by essentials, don't you?"

"No. What?" Kelly asked dubiously. Both of these Texans were enjoying this far too much and it made her wary.

"Deodorant and toilet paper, honey. 'Cause most of the places we go are out in the middle of the boondocks."

She burst into laughter. "Enough for six months, right?"

Coots continued to chuckle. "On second thought, maybe you'd better hire a camel caravan. I can just see it now: rollers for your hair, nail polish, perfume—"

Kelly stifled more laughter. "Okay, I get the point. I'll come to the airport or wherever you want me to meet you with bells on."

"By the way, Sam wanted a few minutes of your time when you were done with us," Coots said, a know-it-all grin on his face.

She shouldn't have blushed, but she did. Hastily picking up her papers and purse to quell her nervous reaction, Kelly answered in a casual voice, "Good. I wanted to thank him for dropping that report off to me last night." Well, that wasn't a total lie. But it wasn't the whole truth, either. Regardless of the outcome of her meeting with Boots and Coots, she had wanted to personally thank Sam for being so supportive.

"He's out in the warehouse with Colly, our mechanic," Boots said, pointing toward the door that led outside.

Kelly nodded and set off down the carpeted hall. At the

very end, between the richly furnished offices, was a floor to ceiling photograph of a huge oil well fire. Plumes of billowing red, yellow and orange flames were exploding skyward from the desert well. Above were frighteningly black clouds of smoke. She shuddered inwardly, remembering that it was Blanchard pipe that had failed under just such a circumstance and had left two men injured. Taking a deep breath, Kelly made a turn and walked out into the high humidity and Texas sunlight.

She had purposefully dressed in burgundy slacks and a simple, no-nonsense pink blouse with her hair drawn back into a chignon at the nape of her neck. She had found through hard experience that businessmen responded to her more as an equal if she wore pants rather than a dress. Kelly shook her head over the stupidity of it all. She had a brain in her head regardless of what she wore! Tendrils of hair curled softly about her face from the dampness in the air as she ducked into the coolness of the large, clean warehouse. Kelly halted, allowing her eyes to adjust to the sudden shade.

"Well, how did it go?" a male voice inquired from behind her.

Kelly gasped and turned on her heel. She met Sam Tyler's interested gaze, her heart beginning to pound at his curious scrutiny.

"I . . . uh . . . God, you scared me! Do you always sneak up on people?" she demanded breathlessly, resting her slender fingers at the base of her throat.

His white coveralls were marked with dark smudges of grease. The same hands Kelly remembered as being gentle despite their size and strength were now smeared with machine oil. He was carrying a large coupling in his left hand; his right arm was still in the sling. Sam's blue eyes twinkled as he held her startled gaze. "Sorry." His smile became more devastating. "I try not to make a habit of scaring beautiful women."

Kelly took a step back from him. The bright sun slanted off his broad shoulders, making Tyler seem even taller and more well muscled than she recalled. It was her imagination. She blinked, gathering her wits together. "Boots said you wanted to see me," she explained abruptly, nervous beneath his blue eyes.

Sam moved next to her. "Follow me. We can talk as we walk. Colly will throw a wrench at me if I don't get this coupling over to him."

Kelly nodded and fell in step with him. She was grateful when he shortened his stride for her sake. Although she was long-legged, she was no match for Sam's stride. "I wanted to come out and thank you," she said in a rush of words. Why did he make her feel edgy? The coveralls he wore zipped up the front of his chest and she couldn't help but stare at the mass of black hair visible above the zipper. He was excruciatingly masculine.

"I'd like to talk with you privately, if I could," she said, glancing up at him.

"No problem." He looked at his watch. "It's noon. Why don't I get cleaned up a little and I'll take you over to Pondi's, a great seafood restaurant not far from here." He smiled. "Besides, you need some meat on your bones, Kelly Blanchard. You're too damn skinny for a Texas woman."

She thrilled inwardly to the way her name rolled off his tongue. Frowning and trying not to show that he was affecting her so deeply, she shrugged. "How would you know if I were skinny or not?" she challenged, on guard against the familiarity that just naturally seemed to exist between them.

"Remember, I was the guy that held you last night." There was teasing in his tone. "And as I recall, I could feel every rib. Now, you willing to own up to being underweight and let me buy you lunch? Or are you going to fight me every inch of the way?"

An unwilling smile curved her lips. "Okay, Sam Tyler, I'll take your browbeating this one time. I owe you, anyway."

3

After Kelly was introduced to Colly, a huge man who was much more heavily muscled than Sam, they departed. Kelly let Sam drive them in one of the many white Cadillacs that belonged to the company. The air conditioning was a lovely respite from the heat and Kelly relaxed in the comfort of the car as Sam drove.

"Does everyone at Boots and Coots own a Cadillac?" she asked drily.

"They're our company cars."

"Some company car," she complimented, trying not to smile with him.

"You figure that our expenses run a minimum of several hundred thousand dollars a day for a team to go on a blowout. Most blowouts aren't capped or killed right away. Boots went on one that took six months to extinguish. Add the money up on that."

Kelly did some quick arithmetic. "No wonder all you guys go around driving Cadillacs and wearing eighteen carat gold Rolex watches!"

"Money doesn't buy everything."

Kelly met his teasing blue gaze. "You're right. Money never did buy my Dad or myself."

"Didn't think so."

"Oh?"

He slowed the car down and pulled into the parking lot of the restaurant. "I'd hate to be the man to make the mistake of trying to buy you," he laughed. "You'd probably deck him."

Kelly shot him a prim look. "I am a feminist, Mr. Tyler. But I don't think it's necessary to go around clubbing people to make myself understood."

Sam enjoyed her quicksilver moodiness. One moment her green eyes sparkled with challenge; the next, with an angry golden flame of righteousness. "Okay," he said, "I give up!" He got out and then leaned down. "I'll be an MCP and open the car door for you."

He was impossible! Kelly broke into laughter. "Okay, I give up too! Please, open the door for me. Despite this liberated day and age, I always have room for a gentleman in my life."

His hand fitted perfectly in the small of her back as he guided her toward the restaurant. He stole a look down at her as he opened the door. She looked a hundred percent better than yesterday. "Tell me," he murmured, "do you look great today because of a night's sleep or me holding you?"

She shivered imperceptibly at the husky tone of his voice. Kelly had been unable to wipe Sam Tyler from her mind. And he knew she was attracted to him! Not wanting to give him an edge, she muttered, "I slept well, if you insist upon knowing."

Sam guided her to a darkened booth. His clean white coveralls almost glowed in the dimly lit atmosphere of the restaurant. Shadows played across his face as he sat there watching her. He folded his large, callused hand around the glass of water the waitress set before him. Many small and some larger scars covered his fingers and the back of his hand. It was mute testimony to working around machinery and welding all of his adult life.

"I'm going to take the liberty of ordering lunch for you, Ms. Blanchard."

She stared at him. "As a show of male force?"

A grin edged his strong mouth. "No, just so you can benefit from my good taste. Although—" he looked down at his coveralls—"you'd never know I have any taste from my present outfit."

If he had said it any other way, she might have taken issue with his statement. "Let's see what your taste is worth, Mr. Tyler," she challenged softly.

"Okay. I think you'll be pleased."

After he gave the waitress their order, Sam became serious. His brows drew together slightly. "You look pretty happy compared to yesterday. Something good must have come out of that meeting with Boots and Coots this morning."

She nodded, sipping the vodka gimlet she had ordered. "They've agreed to give me one more chance," she explained. "I'm going to go on the next call." She saw his face tense. "What's wrong?"

He turned his cold mug of beer around in his hand, saying nothing for a moment. "They're going to let you go on our next call?"

"Yes."

"What if it's to South America? Or to the Persian Gulf?"

"I don't care where it is, Sam. I've got to see Blanchard pipe under field conditions. I want to be there in case something happens. I refuse to let one more person be hurt in the field because of our pipe. That's a promise I made to myself."

He watched her through hooded eyes. She had backbone. More than most men. "You're still a woman in a man's world, Kelly. God, I'd hate to think of the reaction of the Saudis if they saw you over there with us."

Her emerald eyes flashed with fire. "Since when did God hand out brains just to men and not to women? I've been running the eastern region of Blanchard Pipe for the last seven years for my father. I know this business inside out from the regional level. The salesmen I deal with don't care whether I wear a dress or pants." That was a lie. But she didn't care. Sam had picked a sore point with her and she would not apologize for her explosiveness on the topic. "I was born in Texas. I was raised around wildcat wells, roughnecks and this crazy industry of ours. Just because I moved to Pittsburgh when I married, that doesn't rob me of my knowledge of the oil fields." Her voice became less strident, more introspective. "My father's name is solid in this business, Sam. I aim to carry on in the same fine tradition. I won't have his reputation blackened by anything or anyone. And especially not by some male chauvinists who think that because I'm a woman I'm a harebrained idiot!"

"Hey," he called softly, catching her startled gaze,

"I'm on your side, Kelly. I believe in you. I'm just a little worried about some of the regions we might get called into. We'll really be roughing it."

Kelly sat up and squared her shoulders. "I don't want to sound egotistical, Sam, but if I could survive the last year of my life in one piece, I can survive anything." Her voice grew husky. "I had a husband who wanted to break me because I didn't fit his idea of what a woman should be. Gage Wallace was trying to oust my ex-husband from their partnership. And on top of that, my father died a week ago." Her lips thinned as she looked beyond him, fighting back tears. "Don't worry about me surviving in the wilderness. That will be a piece of cake compared to everything else that has happened."

He pulled a white handkerchief from his back pocket and placed it between them. "You know what I like about you?"

Kelly took the handkerchief and dabbed at her eyes. "No. According to Todd, no man in his right mind would like anything about me. I'm too assertive. Too head-strong. Too—"

"I happen to applaud all those attributes," he interrupted, catching the wariness in her eyes. "You're a Texan. That says it all as far as I'm concerned. Your ex couldn't have been born here."

She returned the damp handkerchief. "No, he came from a very rich steel family in Pennsylvania."

"Any children?"

Kelly shook her head. "No."

"Ever want a family?"

She managed a wry grimace. "Yes, if I can ever find a man who will be happy with me as I am."

Sam allowed a hint of a smile. She was a woman who knew herself and had been unwilling to accept other people's assessments of her abilities and talents. Now, she was wary of any male. "Don't give up on all of us just yet," he coaxed.

The waitress brought their lunch, interrupting their conversation. Sam was pleased with Kelly's reaction to the Monk fish.

"It tastes like lobster!" she exclaimed.

"They call it 'poor man's lobster.'"

Kelly laughed. "You can't be exactly poor working for Boots and Coots."

"No, I'm not. But then, I don't count happiness in terms of money, either."

She was pleased with his answer. After barely eating during the last seven days, she was suddenly famished. Sam was right, she acknowledged, she was terribly underweight. Later they lingered over a light wine. Finally Kelly roused herself.

"How are you feeling?"

"The burns? Fine. Another five days and I can get rid of this damn sling."

"I feel awful about—"

"You've apologized already," he admonished.

Her brows knitted. "I wish it hadn't happened. Getting burned scares me worse than anything."

Sam allowed a dry smile. "That's why you're not a firefighter and I am."

"Fire scares me for a lot of reasons," she admitted.

Sam heard a touch of fear in her voice. "Something happened?"

Kelly nodded. "When I was twelve our house burned, Sam. I can remember waking up in the middle of the night coughing and choking. I could see the red glow outside my bedroom door and I panicked. I remember two firefighters in oxygen masks climbing through a window and finding me hiding in the closet. I was hysterical.''

He drew in a deep breath. "You're damn lucky you didn't die of smoke inhalation. That was a close call.''

"Too close," she agreed. Why was she admitting all her worst fears to him? They talked as if they had been friends for a million years. Who was this man who sat across from her? she wondered. "Tell me about yourself, Sam. Were you born in Texas?''

"Yes, ma'am. Little place in West Texas called Del Rio.''

"And your family?''

"My mother's still alive. I have two younger sisters.''

"No one else?'' Why should she care whether he was married or not? But she did. Unconsciously, Kelly held her breath, waiting for him to answer.

"There used to be," he admitted with a sigh. He made a grimace. "Unfortunately, Fay couldn't deal with my life as a firefighter.''

Kelly felt guilty for prying that information out of him. Sam Tyler's personal life was no business of hers. She shouldn't have forced him to look back on that kind of agony. "I'm sorry," she apologized. "Sometimes my curiosity gets the better of me.''

"That's all right. I expect a woman like you to ferret out whatever interests her.''

She lifted her chin, meeting, holding his azure gaze. "Tell me," she asked, "are you always so gentle with people who have hoof-and-mouth disease?''

A grin crept back onto his face. "With most people, I am. Why?"

She gave a small shrug. "I wish I had some of your patience and understanding of people. You had every right to tell me to mind my own business."

Sam took the check, pulled out his credit card and handed them both to the waitress. A glimmer of humor remained in the depths of his eyes. "Well, you're bound to find out sooner or later anyway."

Perplexed, Kelly asked, "What are you talking about?"

Sam signed the credit card receipt and thanked the waitress. He returned his attention to her. "Anyone ever connected with me knows I have a decided weakness for redheads. I love redheaded women."

She stared blankly at him for a long moment. Then her lips thinned. "Is that a statement or a challenge?"

Sam grasped her elbow and helped her to stand. He guided her noiselessly out of the restaurant. Despite the large roughout boots he wore, he made no sound on the tiled floor. "Take it any way you want, Kelly Blanchard," he taunted, his mouth near her ear.

Kelly shivered inwardly at the purr in his voice. She pulled her elbow from his grasp, giving him a sharp glance. "Why do I have the feeling you're the cat and I'm the mouse?"

Sam laughed softly as he opened the door for her. "I just hope that when the next fire call comes in, I'm chosen for the team. It will be interesting to watch a redheaded woman dealing with that kind of stressful situation. My bet's on you, by the way."

She couldn't help smiling. His teasing was without rancor. Sam Tyler, in his own special way, was boosting her confidence. If there was a mean bone in his body, she didn't know where it might exist. He was so different from Todd. Different and refreshing.

It was late Saturday morning and Kelly didn't want to work anymore. She sat in the cozy breakfast nook surrounded by several hanging green plants. A smile crossed her lips. Her father had always loved greenery of any kind and his house certainly attested to that. Along the sills of each window were a myriad of bright, flowering plants ranging from cactus to African violets.

Moments later, her father's housekeeper bustled in with a breakfast tray. "And here you are working, Miss Blanchard!" Hattie chided, placing a plate filled with eggs, bacon and potatoes in front of her. "Come on now, don't give me that look! You need to eat!"

"This is too much food!" Kelly protested lamely.

Hattie, who had been her father's housekeeper for almost thirty years, patted Kelly's shoulder. "Now you look here, Missy, you eat! And I don't want another word from you until then. Just put all of this paperwork aside and stuff yourself."

Kelly did what she could, but she barely made a dent in the delicious food. When Hattie returned she glared at the half-filled plate and grudgingly replaced it with a cup of steaming coffee.

"Just like your father," Hattie grumbled, and then marched off to the kitchen once again.

Kelly rested her head against her hand, staring out the window. It was lovely outside. She could spot a blue jay bickering with a blackbird in the trees around the swimming pool. Glancing at the stack of work before her, Kelly forced herself to get busy. Her head wasn't into it, and her heart . . . well, that was lingering on Sam Tyler. It shouldn't be, she told herself sternly. But it was.

With a sigh, she opened up the first document and forced herself to begin reading.

The doorbell chimed. Kelly looked toward the kitchen. Hattie stuck her head out the entrance, puzzlement written on her dark features.

"You expect'n anyone, Missy?"

Kelly shook her head, then glanced at her wristwatch. It was ten-thirty A.M. "No. Were you?"

"No, ma'am," she said, marching through the breakfast nook and down the hall to the foyer.

Kelly's heart leaped. Sam Tyler? No, it couldn't be. But . . . it was his voice! She roused herself and stared down toward the foyer. Concerned, she tugged her apricot-colored silk robe more closely around her and rose.

Sam's bulk filled the hall. Kelly smiled, meeting his azure gaze. Her heart lifted in silent joy and she didn't try to quell the breathless anticipation that filled her. Today he was in a light beige cowboy shirt with the sleeves rolled up on his forearms. His jeans were molded to the length of his legs, accentuating his well-muscled thighs.

"I happened to be in this neck of the woods and thought I'd drop over and see how you're coming along," he said.

"Hattie, bring Mr. Tyler some coffee, please." She gestured to the other wrought-iron chair. "Sit down," she invited. She could feel the heat staining her cheeks, but there was nothing that could be done to hide that fact. It had been years since Kelly had blushed so easily! And yet, Sam Tyler looked so devastatingly virile and handsome that it almost took her voice away. No man had ever affected her so strongly in her life.

Sam sat carefully in the delicate-looking piece of furniture. He gave her a quick smile. "I haven't heard from you lately."

"I've been up to my neck with my father's business."

He gave a casual nod of his head. "Your father was known to be a workaholic. Are you turning into one also?" he probed.

Hattie brought the coffee and gave Sam a warm smile. "Here you go, Mr. Tyler."

Sam took the fragile china cup in his large, callused hands. "Thank you." He waited until the housekeeper had left. "You planning on working today?"

Kelly nodded, gesturing toward the pile of documents spread in front of her on the small table. "Unfortunately, yes." She tilted her head. An inexplicable happiness was bubbling up within her. She could lose herself in the blueness of his eyes, in that crooked, teasing smile on his sensual mouth and in the balm of his husky voice. "Why?"

He shrugged. "Oh, I kind of had other plans for you today," he hedged, watching her carefully.

"You did?"

Sam enjoyed the sparkle that appeared in her jade eyes. She still looked pale and drawn. But that did not mar her attractiveness in the least. The impulse to simply reach over and run his fingers through her silken hair was almost a tangible urge. He forced himself back to his purpose for coming. "We figured since you'll be coming with us on a call, someone had better acquaint you with the equipment plus other odds and ends."

"That someone being you?"

"Any objections?"

Kelly forced a cool smile. He had given her a confident grin. One that said: of course you won't have any objections. "Are you always so sure of yourself?"

Sam tried to look contrite. "Caught again. What do you have against a man who is sure of himself, Kelly Blanchard?"

It was her turn to quell a burgeoning grin. "Nothing . . . everything."

Sam toyed with the cup of coffee between his hands. "Care to tell me more about it over lunch?"

"Is that an invitation or an order?"

"Where you're concerned, an invitation." His blue eyes sparkled with a mischievous glint. "You don't give orders to redheads and live to tell about it. Strictly an invitation."

Kelly rose, her laughter ringing down the hall. My God, how long had it been since she had laughed so freely? The thought made her suddenly sober. Embarrassed that Sam had caught her in a quixotic mood, she swept past him. "I'll be out in fifteen minutes," she promised.

Actually, it took twenty-five. But Sam would understand. She deliberated over what to wear—something she hadn't done in a long time. Todd hadn't cared what she wore as long as it wasn't jeans or pants. But she had been raised in them. Today she fingered a pair of well-worn designer jeans. To hell with it, she decided, jeans it would be! It would be hot and muggy out in the Texas sunlight so she chose a cool apple green tanktop.

Throwing her hair up in a delightful spill of curls high on her head, she knew she would be as cool as it was possible to be. The morning had suddenly brightened for Kelly. She tried not to look at the reason for her new joy. Right now there was no room in her life for another man. Todd had taught her too well. . . .

4

Boots thought it might be helpful to give you a quick lesson in the type of equipment we use at a blowout," Sam explained, guiding her out the back door of the main office. He was having a devil of a time keeping his voice even, his eyes where they were supposed to be and his hands at his sides. Kelly was a woman in every sense of the word. He liked her easy, fluid walk, the intelligent spark in her eyes and that steeltrap mind she possessed. Did she know how unique she was? He compressed his lips, wanting to convey many of his impressions about her. It might give her spirit a lift. Even with a light application of makeup she still appeared pale. His mind drifted back. His own father had died unexpectedly of a heart attack out on a drilling rig and he felt once again the pain he was sure Kelly was experiencing. Placing a hand beneath her elbow, he guided her toward the first row of spotless white equipment.

"Over here is our basic tool at a blowout. This is called an Athey Wagon." He halted near it. "Basically, it's a sixty-foot boom and hook assembled on a set of bulldozer type tracks."

Kelly looked up at a long arm with a huge hook at the end of it. She was wildly aware of Sam's nearness. It was simultaneously heady, frightening and exciting. Trying to appear nonchalant, she gave a brief nod of her head. "What do you do with this ungainly looking thing?"

Sam grinned. "We use a bulldozer with galvanized sheets protecting the operator to push the athey wagon into the fire. Once there, the hook is lowered and then we begin to pull the mangled steel debris off the platform."

Kelly looked up at him. In the strong Texas sun, he looked incredibly masculine—a cowboy torn from a bygone era, the 1800s, and placed in this day and age. All he needed was a cowboy hat. Instead, he wore the perennial Boots and Coots white baseball cap. It was placed at a rakish angle on his dark hair, the bill protecting his narrowed eyes from the sunlight. "Is it necessary to get rid of all the rigging before you go in to put out the fire?" she wanted to know.

"Can't start until we do. That's why the athey wagon is a must. After clearing away the debris from the platform and surrounding area, we use the wagon to place the explosive charges into the flame."

Kelly shuddered. "It sounds dangerous."

Sam smiled patiently. "Only if you don't know what you're doing."

Blowouts of any kind—with or without fire—were killers. Unconsciously, she rubbed her arms in silent disagreement. "I know you fly all over the world to put out fires. How does all this equipment get over to say, Saudi Arabia or to South America?"

"By plane," Sam explained, leading her over to a specially built truck. "We use these trucks to load our wagons, the pumps and piperacks into the plane."

"Do you have a plane?"

"No, the oil or gas company that calls us usually provides one. It might be privately owned or a commercial jet. Just depends upon the circumstance."

"And inside North America?"

"We usually truck the equipment in, if possible."

Sam took her inside the huge twelve-thousand-foot warehouse. "In here we keep our piperack skids." He stopped at the first immaculately painted piperack. "And naturally, as you can see, Blanchard Pipe is on it."

Kelly nodded, noting that the white twenty-foot-long pieces of pipe were neatly stacked on the outside of the unit. She was amazed at the economy and utilization of space. The inside of the unit was a storehouse for large tools and parts. She poked her head inside one, finding an array of adapters, spanner wrenches, nozzles and various other tools she couldn't identify. Sam patiently explained everything to her in layperson's language.

Afterward, she stood at the mouth of the warehouse, her gaze traveling over the foam units, the pumps and piperacks. "It's impressive," she stated quietly.

Sam nodded, hands resting on his hips. "More impressive because everything you see here was designed and built by our own men at Boots and Coots." Her eyes widened at his remark and he felt as though he might fall into their warm, inviting depths. "Remember, every man here at Boots and Coots is a specialist, Kelly. We have some who are designers, others who are ace welders, mud specialists, foam specialists. The list goes on but I don't want to bore you with how good we are.''

Kelly grinned. ''No humble pie here at Boots and Coots, is there?''

''Not a crumb. When you're good, you're damn good.''

''And you're the best.''

Sam gave a satisfied nod of his head and led her back toward the air-conditioned coolness of the main office. ''We get an average of sixty calls a year from around the world, so we can't be too bad at what we do.''

''Sixty?'' she murmured. Walking back into the office, Kelly took a deep breath. With the Texas humidity of the Gulf Coast region, air conditioning was always a welcome blessing. She glanced up as Sam led her out toward the front desk. ''That keeps you pretty busy, doesn't it?''

''A little,'' he admitted.

She frowned. Would she like her husband to be gone that much of the time each year? Kelly caught herself. What in the world was she thinking about! Upbraiding herself, she shoved the ridiculous thought out of her head. She became aware of Sam's hand on her arm. It provoked a pleasant tingling sensation in her arm.

''How about lunch? I'm starved.''

Kelly hesitated. She enjoyed Sam's company. He was good for her bruised, battered spirit. Yet . . .

''Tell you what,'' Sam added, ''you haven't been back in Texas long. How about if I take you to a good down-home place where they make some of the best ribs you've ever eaten? You can't tell me you aren't starved for some good Texas grub.''

She opened her mouth and then closed it. ''Has

anyone ever told you that you could sell an igloo to an Eskimo, Mr. Tyler?" she asked.

Sam gave her an irresistible look. "Just my charming personality, Ms. Blanchard."

Kelly had to stifle a smile as she settled back in the luxury of the white Cadillac. Today she felt like a child but dare she show it? "Are you always so affable?" she demanded.

Sam gazed at her momentarily. "Usually. Why?" And then a twinkle came to his azure eyes. He leaned back and placed his right arm behind her shoulders—not touching her, but very close. He saw her eyes widen. In a deliberate motion, he briefly touched her cheek. Her skin was warm and pliant beneath his fingers. "There, does that confirm your suspicions that I'm out to get you?"

Kelly swallowed hard, alarmed at the wonderful sensation created by his fingers negligently stroking her flesh. She turned so her back was against the door and she was as far away from him as she could get within the confines of the car. "What are you talking about?" she demanded. Her voice sounded ridiculously wispy. How could his touch evoke such a physical reaction from her? Kelly felt her hands growing damp and quickly put them in her lap.

Sam withdrew his arm and studied her from beneath his thick, dark lashes. "Let's level with one another, Kelly," he began, his voice soft, cajoling. "I find you attractive, intelligent and damned exciting. You're like no other woman I've ever met."

Fear surged through her. "I'm not up to playing whatever games you've got in mind, Sam."

"Why do you think I'm playing a game?" he asked quietly.

Kelly struggled with a number of different retorts. "You wouldn't understand!"

"Try me."

"No."

"Why?"

"Because you're a man. And men don't understand!"

Sam was aware of the intense emotion behind her blurted words. At that second, she looked so damned vulnerable and yet she was defiant too. Ever since he'd met her, he had searched his memory for scraps of information on her ex-husband, Todd Chandler. Todd had been an unwitting pawn of Gage Wallace's. Chandler was known within the industry as a weakling. He was also known as a manipulator, although he lacked the finesse of a man like Wallace. As he studied Kelly, Sam wondered how Chandler had manipulated her feelings and emotions to make her distrustful of every man who might want to know her on a more personal level.

"You don't think a man can be honest, Kelly?" he prodded gently.

She gave a stubborn shake of her head.

"Because of your ex-husband?"

Bitterness tinged her voice. "Yes."

"Any other man cause you to see all the rest of us in such an unfavorable light?"

Her anger slowly abated. Kelly slumped back against the seat, eyes cast downward. "I owe you an apology," she admitted quietly. And then she raised her chin and her flawless eyes met his azure gaze. "I'm jumpy, Sam. Todd wasn't to be trusted—with anything. He took advantage of every opportunity to put me down."

"He wanted to mold you to fit his image of the perfect wife?"

"Yes. That way, I guess I was less threatening to him."
Tears suddenly filled her eyes and she opened her hands
in a silent plea. "Tell me, Sam, what is wrong with a
woman trying to become her whole self? Why should I
have to be a puppet or a reflection of some man's ideals.
Why can't I be myself?"

He reached out, gently running his fingers along her
shoulder in a soothing motion. "Maybe I can put it into
better perspective for you, Kelly."

She dashed the tears from her eyes. "I wish somebody
would."

He gave her a tender look. "There are two types of
males in the world, honey. One type are boys who grew
into adult bodies but never left their immaturity, their
brittle egos or childish games behind them. They're the
type of men who see women like yourself as a decided
threat." He caressed the nape of her neck, watching her
visibly relax beneath his ministrations. "They might call
you a tomboy, a feminist or macho. And by doing it,
they're showing their own stunted growth."

"But we women pay for their immaturity!"

"Yes, but you're going to have to persevere, Kelly.
What choice do you have? If you want to explore your
full potential, you have to doggedly bow your head and
keep going. You can't go back to what Todd tried to mold
you into. You can't stand still. I think you're too excited
by life to stand idly by." His heart melted as her emerald
eyes shone with the light of new discovery. It thrilled him
to simply sit and exchange ideas and philosophies with
her. She was a woman who was passionately emotional
and yet intelligent too. "Anyway," he went on in his
Texas drawl, "the second type of male is a true adult. He

is a person who is comfortable with himself, Kelly. He sees the world in subtler shades of gray than the boys. That type of man enjoys a woman who is getting in touch with herself. A mature man doesn't find a woman such as yourself a threat." He allowed a smile to tug at his mouth. "We see life as an adventure. One that we'd like to share with such a woman. . . ."

Kelly stared at Sam. She had the distinct feeling he was talking directly to her about how he felt. Texas men were notorious for their chauvinism. But Sam was a breed apart. "I think you're as different and unique as I am."

Sam smiled and brushed the back of his hand across her cheek. "We have the time to find out, don't we?"

Kelly nodded hesitantly, uncertain of all these new, unexpected feelings she was experiencing.

"Now do you understand that when I say I find you attractive, intelligent and exciting it doesn't just mean I want to take you to bed?"

She felt heat sweeping across her neck and up into her face. "You do have a way with words, Tyler," she shot back.

Sam grinned, starting up the car. "I think you prize honesty above everything else, Kelly Blanchard. And I intend always to be honest with you."

She settled back and put on her seat belt. They drove in silence, leaving the sprawling skyline of Port Neches and then Houston in the distance. Kelly sat there digesting his words. He wanted her, but on all levels. Suddenly, her wariness of Sam evaporated. Taking a deep breath, she looked over at him as he drove.

"How old are you?"

"Thirty-five. Why?"

"I was just wondering what it took for you to see women differently than most men do," Kelly provided in explanation.

"A set of parents that encouraged me and my sisters to do whatever we set our minds to. My father didn't make a distinction between the children when a tire on the car had to be changed or something mechanical had to be fixed."

"So your sisters are . . ." She groped for the correct word.

"Feminists? Yes, I would say they are. One is a veterinarian and the other is teaching computer science at a local college." His blue eyes twinkled. "They remind me a lot of you: headstrong, courageous and outspoken."

"And you don't find that a problem?"

"Why are any of those qualities a problem, Kelly?"

"Most men see them that way. That's why."

"Do you think maybe you're a little prejudiced about men in general?"

Kelly gave a weak smile. "*Touché*, Sam Tyler. *Touché*."

"No one is keeping score," he reminded her darkly.

"Thanks," she whispered, "I needed to know that."

Sam reached out, capturing her hand for just a moment and giving it a reassuring squeeze. "I know."

Her fingers tingled where his hand had briefly rested. A crazy thought tore through her: what would it be like to be loved by Sam? If he was this understanding in conversation, he must be just as sensitive in lovemaking. Kelly blushed furiously over those thoughts. "Who developed your appreciation of women as real people?" she asked.

"Like I said, it began with my parents. My mother had plenty to do with opening my eyes to the fact that women really weren't the weaker of the species at all. And then, every woman I knew thereafter more or less honed my appreciation for the sex."

"I'll bet there were plenty," she muttered under her breath, more as a comment to herself than Sam.

"Jealousy doesn't become you," he teased, smiling.

Kelly returned the smile, feeling more free than she had in a long time. "No, it doesn't. And I have a feeling that each woman was very special to you. You don't seem the type to use a woman and then throw her away."

He pursed his lips. "Right again. But then, I look at both men and women in that light, Kelly. Every human being is unique. Of course," he drawled, "redheaded women are just more fascinating than anyone else."

Kelly laughed with him. "For once I'm glad I have red hair."

"So am I," he returned cryptically.

As the afternoon came to a close, Kelly didn't want to return to her father's home. Who could have made going out for barbecued spareribs an adventure? Sam Tyler did. At the door of the house, Kelly turned, looking up at Sam.

"I think you know how wonderful today has been," she said.

Sam came to a stop, inches separating them. "I can say the same. Want to do it again sometime soon?"

Kelly grinned, touching her stomach. "At least not for another week! I stuffed myself on those delicious ribs. I guess I just never realized how much I had missed Texas food."

He reached out and touched one of her curls. The sun glinted through the trees, leaving a pattern of dappled light on her head. "Do you realize," he began huskily, "that in this light your hair is red, gold and copper?"

His intimate comment made her heart pound unexpectedly. All day she had wanted to rest against his stalwart body and be held. Sam seemed to sense that her grief made her more vulnerable. More in need of someone. But not just anyone. Him. Kelly gazed up, meeting, holding Sam's gaze. Her heart soared, her body responded as he drew his hand down her cheek, cupped her chin, and tilted her head up to meet his descending mouth.

His breath was moist against her cheek as she closed her eyes, waiting . . . waiting. A tingle spread through her as his mouth brushed her lips. Touching, testing. He smelled wonderful. His arms slid around her body, drawing her against him. His hands moved down her torso to her hips. A soft moan of surrender sounded in her throat as his mouth moved masterfully across her lips, taking her, making her his in that fiery, breathless moment. Her heart raced wildly as his tongue outlined her lips momentarily, then lightly touched the corners of her mouth.

He gently disengaged his arms. His large hands cradled her face and he deepened the kiss, his tongue seeking entrance to her mouth. She sagged against the hard oak of his body, craving further contact with him.

Slowly, Sam broke the spell of the kiss. His breathing was irregular, his eyes narrowed and dark with desire as he stared down at her in silence. His callused fingers gently caressed her skin.

He frowned, feeling her tremble. He knew that what

they had shared had been mutual. Placing his arms comfortably around her back, he allowed Kelly to reorient herself. "I've been wanting to do that ever since that night I held you," he admitted quietly.

"I have to go, Sam," she said faintly, pushing away from his solid body. Kelly felt him release her and she felt bereft. She tried to keep the hurt out of her voice. "It's been a lovely day—"

"With more to come," he promised.

Her lashes swept upward. Lord, he made her tremble from just his kiss! "Thanks for the day, Sam. I needed it."

He smiled and opened the door for her. "My pleasure. Mind if I give you a call sometime next week so we can share another day together?"

Kelly shakily touched her temple, confused by the myriad of feelings exploding within her. "I won't play games with you, Sam. I do enjoy your company, but right now . . ." She took a deep breath and closed her eyes momentarily. "Right now I'm scared to death. Of you. Of myself."

Sam nodded. "I understand. You want some breathing room."

"Yes."

He leaned down to place a kiss on her hair. "Okay, you've got it, my redheaded witch. You call me when you'd like some company."

5

Kelly glanced at her watch. It was four-thirty P.M. Thank God, the day was almost over. The sight of her watch reminded her of the gold Rolex Sam wore. A sign of good taste. Of class. Had a week and a half gone by since she'd last seen him? She stared sightlessly, wanting nothing more than a hot bath and bed. Filling in for her father had been tougher than she had anticipated. Each day was one scheduled meeting after another with management, supervisors and Blanchard sales personnel to establish new company policy.

She gathered together another sheaf of papers that still needed her signature. Even with the demands of the job, she still found her thoughts returning to Sam Tyler.

Since their luncheon, she had had no word from him. What had she expected? She had been the one to set the rules for their relationship. She knew he was divorced, but she wondered if he was seeing someone else.

Probably a redhead, she thought ruefully, scratching her illegible signature on the last letter. Still, in the emptiness of her Dad's elegant, hollow home, she had wished for his presence. He was easy to talk with and listen to. How vastly different he was from Todd, whose acid tongue and scathing retorts did nothing but increase her own defensiveness. She was glad those days were gone.

"Ms. Blanchard?" Susan called, opening the office door. Her secretary wore an agitated expression.

Before Kelly could answer, Gage Wallace deftly stepped past the secretary. His self-assured smile brought Kelly's blood to a quick boiling point.

"That's all right, Susan," Kelly reassured the distraught woman. "You can leave now. Thank you."

Gage turned, his dark eyes narrowed. In his hand he held a dozen red roses. "I just happened to be in the Houston area for the week, Kelly." He approached her desk and placed the bouquet on it. "I know you'll forgive me for dropping in without notice, but it's almost quitting time. I've made reservations at the Royden Oaks Country Club for us tonight."

Her face grew tight, her emerald eyes flashing with barely contained anger. "You won't give up, will you?" she hissed, clenching her fists at the sides of her lavender dress.

Gage gave her a viperous smile. "You're a little too confident of yourself under the circumstances, Kelly."

The coldness in his voice made her tremble inwardly but she was damned if he was going to know it. She jutted out her chin, placing her hands on her hips.

"You're not making sense—as usual."

"No?" One black brow rose. "As I predicted, word's going around about Blanchard Pipe's failures. You're swimming into some very murky waters, Kelly. If you had any business sense at all, you'd let me buy into your company. I could bail you out with my good name."

She wanted to laugh. And then she wanted to curse him. She leaned forward, hands flat against her desk. "Get this straight, Gage. I want nothing, *nothing* from you! You found a way to get Todd out of your partnership and remove him. You got away with that. But you won't pull that kind of maneuver on me. I wouldn't care if you were the only steel and aluminum manufacturer in the country, I wouldn't buy from you! Do I make myself perfectly clear?"

She was trembling, wanting to strike his too handsome face. Gage Wallace represented everything she hated about big business. He was amoral, competitive to the point of being cutthroat.

Gage smiled, holding her furious gaze. "As usual, you do. I see you haven't stopped shooting straight from the hip, Kelly."

She straightened up. "Don't go playing hurt little boy with me! You can take that poor puppy wounded look and leave."

He tapped one carefully manicured finger on the desk top. "Never did fool you, did I, Kelly?" he asked softly. "You always knew where I was coming from. You know, we would make one hell of a team in the oil and gas industry. The two of us. With your beauty and bravado coupled with my business sense, we could corner the pipe market."

She felt nausea rising in her throat. "What does it take to make you understand I want nothing to do—"

"Kelly . . ."

Her heart pounded wildly as her head snapped up. Sam Tyler stood just inside the door, his face tense. Wallace lost none of his cool as he turned. The silence was tense as the two men glared at one another, shock written on both of their faces.

"Wallace . . ." Tyler snarled in a low, menacing voice. And then his angry blue gaze settled on Kelly. Immediately the anger disappeared. "Kelly, grab your things. We've got a call."

It was as if lightning had struck the office. For a moment Kelly was frozen to the spot. Wallace and Tyler knew one another! How? Where? A hundred fragmented thoughts whirled through her mind. Then she shook herself and walked quickly around the desk and past Wallace. Just as she passed him, he reached out, gripping her upper arm, and swung her around. Her lips parted in surprise. Before she could utter a word of protest she heard Tyler mutter an obscenity.

"I believe the lady made herself clear," Tyler warned. He grabbed Wallace's wrist in a viselike grip. His right arm was now free of the sling, so he had the use of both hands. In one quick, clean motion, he pulled Kelly free. His grip tightened on Wallace's wrist until he saw the pain register in the other man's eyes. "Get your suitcase, Kelly," he rasped, never taking his eyes off Wallace. "I'll meet you at the car in a minute."

Kelly glanced wildly at the men, who were frozen in a silent struggle with one another. The harshness in Sam's voice spurred her into action and she left the room, shutting the door behind her. Hurriedly, she walked down the hall to her secretary, giving last-minute orders. Kelly went to her manager's office and alerted Jake. He took the suitcase she had packed for the occasion and carried it out to the white Cadillac waiting outside.

"Be careful, Kelly," he warned, patting her arm. "And don't worry, I'll hold down the fort here for you," Jake assured her.

Her heart was pounding with . . . what? Fear? Anger? No, fear for Sam. The hatred between the two men had been almost tangible to her. Were they fighting in there? She saw Tyler coming quickly out the doors. His face was ashen, inscrutable.

"Get in," he ordered.

Kelly gave Jake a quick hug and did as she was told. In no time, they were on their way to the Houston International airport. The traffic was heavy, adding to the tension in the car. She felt Sam's anger and was unsure of what to do or say.

Finally, she could no longer stand the brittle atmosphere. "Where are we going?"

Sam's eyes never left the road as he expertly wove his way through the traffic. "Saudi Arabia. The Rub al Khali Desert. It's a big one, Kelly. An H2S gas well." He shot her a cutting glance. "I didn't want you along on this one."

Her eyes widened. "Why not?"

"You've been around the block," came the clipped reply. "H2S gas is poisonous as hell. They've got a flame shooting four hundred feet in the air. That means letting the fire continue to burn so it consumes the noxious gas. The gas will kill everything within a fifty-mile radius if the fire goes out." His blue eyes darkened. "You have no damn business coming on this one."

Anger replaced her nervousness. "I've been around

H2S before, Sam Tyler! And quit yelling at me just because you're angry over something else! Just make damn sure I've got oxygen apparatus and I'll be a good girl and stay out of the way. Does that make you feel any better?" Damn! She shouldn't respond to his anger. When she had first seen him at the door, she'd wanted to throw herself into his arms. He had looked so handsome. So capable. And she had missed him terribly during the past week.

His nostrils flared but he kept his eyes on the traffic. "You're so bullheaded, Kelly. That well's already killed five people! It was blown up by a bunch of border terrorists from the Emirates. We're going into some rough territory and frankly, you should stay home. The Rub al Khali Desert is one of the most desolate places in the world. It's a living hell. You should catch the next fire."

She clenched her hands in her lap. "You can't scare me off, Tyler! Blanchard Pipe will be on the job. And I've got to be there too, to prove that I stand behind my father's product one hundred percent. It's a question of honor. I'm going, even if it kills me."

He gave her a grim look. "Has it ever occurred to you, you redheaded witch, that maybe, just maybe, some people would like to see you alive?" He cursed beneath his breath. "No, I suppose it hasn't. You're so damn quick to don your battle armor and prepare for the next skirmish." His hands tightened on the wheel. "Sometimes you haven't got a brain in your head!"

She sat there, ready to explode. If she had been eighteen, she would have slapped his face without a second thought. But she wasn't eighteen. And she heard the concern for her safety in his voice. Taking several deep breaths, she calmed herself.

It was another ten miles before she trusted herself to speak. As she looked over at Sam, she saw the rugged features of his face. His profile looked as if it had been hewn by the sun, wind and rain. There was nothing compromising about him at all.

"I know you're upset, Sam," she began. "I'll stay out of the way so you won't have to worry about me. I'm not a complete idiot. I've had training on H2S gas wells. My Dad dealt with more of them than I care to think about. I know the dangers."

His expression softened slightly as he slid a glance in her direction. The chignon she normally wore had loosened. He had a momentary urge to pull the rest of the pins free, allowing that red hair of hers to flow across her shoulders. "Did you hear me? I said a terrorist group blew up that well. There are always border disputes between the Arab Emirates and the Saudis. You may be knowledgeable about breathing apparatus and gas wells, Kelly. But you're no match for a sniper's bullet or a band of guerillas who are out to destroy everything around their neighbor's oil and gas wells." His mouth became grim. "I spent two tours in Nam. I know what it's like to get shot at and wounded. You're a woman going into a hostile environment." He clenched his teeth, silent for a minute. He couldn't say anything more. Not yet. It was too soon and maybe too late. How could he tell her that she haunted his dreams every night? And that he never ceased to think about her during his waking hours? He needed time to assuage some of her fears of men, time so that she could come to know him better. Now this whole damn thing in the Middle East had erupted and she was walking into a situation where she might get killed.

Sam tried to ignore the ache in his chest caused by that last thought. She was too vital, too alive to die in such a stupid, wasteful manner. Damn her bullheadedness. Her foolhardiness . . .

By the time they arrived at the airport, the heavy equipment was in the process of being loaded. Kelly remained close to Sam, nearly running to keep up with his long stride. The plane being loaded was a C-130 Hercules painted in the camouflage colors of green, brown and beige. Kelly's skin began to crawl as they drew closer. The shouts, directions and roar of equipment blended in a cacophony of discordant noise to her ears. There were three other men in white coveralls besides Sam. She spotted Boots Hansen immediately, his white baseball cap perched on the back of his head as he consulted with the pilots and navigator of the plane.

Sam gripped her arm, bringing her to a halt. His eyes were still filled with anger as he looked down at her. "Get into your coveralls," he said tightly. "Use that building over there to change." It was a small building away from the main terminal area of the airport. Kelly nodded and picked up her suitcase.

Her fingers trembled slightly as she zipped up the front of the coveralls. She had lost most of the pins in her hair and decided to free it. There was a tension about the entire operation that she could not ignore. Questions whirled through her mind as she quickly walked back across the concrete ramp to the C-130. She spotted Sam conferring with Colly and joined them, waiting for further instructions.

Sam glanced down at her. He drew in a breath, mesmerized by her untamed beauty. Her auburn hair was like red flame set against the crisp whiteness of the uniform. His body tightened with a flood of desire and he wondered for the thousandth time what it would be like to bring her proud, willful spirit into union with himself. His gaze raked her from her booted feet to her glorious mane of hair.

"Give Colly your suitcase. We'll be boarding shortly."

"What about my pipe?"

"Already loaded. Go see for yourself," he said, pointing toward the four-engine prop jet aircraft.

"Sam . . . why is the plane camouflaged? It looks military."

He rested his hands on his hips, his face becoming grimmer. "It's a Saudi government plane. And the gas well is owned by the Saudi government, too. Where we're going, it's a free-fire zone. Those pilots you see over there are under contract with the Saudis."

Kelly looked closely at the crew. "Americans?"

"Mercenaries," he ground out. "Men looking for another war to fight." He turned abruptly, leaving her standing alone on the ramp.

It took several hours to load the two Athey wagons, two integrated piperack units and piperack skids. Two of everything were taken so that in case one unit failed, they would have a backup.

Finally Coots waved Kelly over to join him. "You might as well get aboard, Kelly. They're gonna wind this bird up in about ten minutes." His brown eyes grew worried. "You sure you want to come? Boots ain't so sure that—"

"I'm very sure, Coots. I'll stay out of the way. I know

about H2S gas. I won't be a burden to you. I promise." Over the past few hours, Kelly had felt the grim tension in the men, and it frightened her, as did the military nature of the operation. On the other hand, Sam's desire to leave her home, where it was safe, roused her fighting spirit.

Coots took the cap off his head and scratched his brown hair for a moment. "The government has assured us the area's secure from the terrorist faction that blew up that gas well. I don't know . . ."

"Have you gone into unsafe areas before?"

"We've gone into hostile environments when the government we're working for can guarantee our security. If they can't guarantee it, we don't go. Hell, that's why those wells over in Iran and Iraq are still burning. Ain't no one in their right mind gonna try to cap 'em in the middle of that situation."

"But this is different?"

Coots threw the cap back on his head. "They say it is. But I don't believe 'em." He put his arm around her shoulder, walking her toward the gargantuan cargo plane. "I was a tail-gunner aboard B-17's during World War II. I got shot at plenty." He shook his head. "I've seen enough killing to last me ten lifetimes. My gut says the place isn't that secure. I dunno . . ."

Worriedly, Kelly looked up at him. Coots was a large man with broad shoulders, much like Sam. The fact that he hugged her as they walked made her feel like she suddenly had a second father. There was a protective quality about Coots Matthews that made her feel safe. Almost as safe as when Sam held her.

The three American mercenaries watched Kelly's

progress as she climbed up the long ramp at the rear of the plane. She was acutely conscious of their stares. Everywhere she looked, huge skids of firefighting equipment were anchored to the floor of the C-130. Rope cargo netting and nylon webbing hung against the walls of the plane.

"Kelly . . ."

It was Sam's voice—less authoritative, more coaxing. She raised her head and caught sight of him standing by the starboard bulkhead near a row of seats. They weren't passenger plane seats by any means, but she went to him and tried to make herself comfortable against the nylon webbing that provided the only back support. Her pulse was pounding unevenly. Was it because of Sam's closeness? Her fear of starting this journey? Or a combination of both?

"Strap in. They'll be revving up for takeoff." He instantly regretted the coldness in his tone. She looked like a scared little girl. He reached out, making contact with her hand. "I'm sorry I was rough on you earlier," he said gruffly, and then he released her cool fingers.

Kelly felt as if she were in an alien world. The entire rear ramp yawned closed, the groaning of the hydraulics reverberating throughout the bottom of the aircraft. Huge, shadowed equipment loomed above them, with very little space left for anyone to move. The voices of the men competed with the screeching, whistling sound of the four mighty prop jet engines.

Kelly swallowed and found her throat was dry. Her eyes were wide, betraying her inner fears. What was she getting herself into? Sam's hand slid over hers, giving her fingers a reassuring squeeze. His hand was warm. Hers was ice cold. She met his gaze. This time there was no anger in his face. This time there was only concern and tenderness in those wonderful azure eyes.

"Th–thanks," she whispered, meaning it.

Sam gave her a crooked smile. "A little fear is good for you, Kelly," he advised.

The C-130 began to move and she gripped Sam's hand tightly for a moment, adjusting to the new sensations. Boots was moving around the skids, double checking to make sure they were securely fastened to the deck. If the load shifted it could slide into the bulkhead, crushing a human being.

Sam began to gently massage her hand. "Relax," he coaxed. "This part is a piece of cake."

"Yeah?" she mouthed.

His smile deepened. "Yeah." He reached across with his other hand and picked up a thick strand of her hair. "Try and relax," he murmured.

"I'm scared to death," she admitted. The C-130 was gathering speed and as it hit each bump and depression in the taxiway, the plane wallowed like a beached whale.

"Like I said," Sam murmured, "a little fear is good for you."

"I thought that was just your way of getting even with me for coming along."

Sam shook his head. "I may be upset that you're coming, Kelly, but I wouldn't deliberately be cruel to you. The reason I said a little fear is good is because it will keep you alert and on your toes. And where we're going, you don't want to take anything or anyone for granted."

"Wonderful."

Sam switched hands, placing his arm around her

shoulders and continuing to hold her one hand. "You mean even a redhead has a limit on courage?" he teased.

"You," she said, giving him a gentle jab in the ribs, "can be replaced."

He laughed. It was a wonderfully free, uninhibited laugh that rolled through the bowels of the plane. Suddenly she relaxed in his embrace. "On second thought, maybe you can't be," she admitted.

"Glad to hear that, honey."

She made a face. "You sure are confident of yourself, Tyler. Where did they dig you up?"

"I'm confident where you're concerned," he told her in a disturbingly low voice which sent a shiver through her.

The C-130's engines were now changing pitch. The plane suddenly came to a halt and Kelly clutched at Sam's arm.

"It's okay," he soothed. "We're at the beginning of the runway. The pilots are waiting for clearance from the tower. You'll hear them winding up the engines even more, so relax."

She closed her eyes, suddenly grateful for his explanations. "I owe you one, Sam Tyler," she told him earnestly, meeting his stare.

"Yes, and I intend to collect."

The turbo-prop engines began to scream like shrill banshees. The plane vibrated, shivering like an eagle crying to be released from its earthly imprisonment. Sam's arm tightened around her, holding her close as the plane began its forward momentum. Lights dimmed and blinked, leaving them all in the shadows. They were surrounded by the shrill noise, the rattling and clanking of pipe vibrating on the skids. It seemed like forever before the plane broke contact with the runway and fought its way skyward into the gathering dusk. Shakily, Kelly released a long-held breath.

"I'm so glad you're here," she confided to Sam.

He gave her one of his boyish grins. "Me too. Say, you know this could become a pleasant habit. You're kind of nice to hold, my redhaired witch."

He released her hand and disengaged his arm from around her shoulders. He unstrapped himself from the seat and got up. "Stay here. I'm going to steal a thermos of coffee and some food from Boots."

She was more than happy to remain in one place. Apparently the lights in the rear of the plane weren't working properly. Kelly wondered if they would reach the Middle East in one piece. By the way Boots and Coots were acting, they would. Everyone was up, wandering around, checking the cables securing the skids. Sam came back with a thermos and a brown bag. He handed her the bag.

"Here. Dinner."

Kelly was surprised at how hungry she had become. Darkness came quickly as the aircraft headed in an easterly direction. They ate chicken sandwiches and drank black coffee, sharing the one available cup. Even in the dim light, Kelly could see the strain written on Sam's face.

"You're worried, aren't you?"

Sam collected the wrappers and stuffed them back into the bag. "About your being here, yes."

"But not for yourself?"

"No." He held her gaze. "This is a man's job and only

men are going to be present, Kelly. I know it's a chauvinistic statement, but it's not meant to be. You're going into a part of the world where women are considered little more than baby-bearers or merchandise to be sold into harems." His voice lowered. "Maybe it would be wise for you to gather up all your hair and tuck it inside one of those white hard hats we all wear when we're at a site. Boots had an idea."

She felt tiredness creeping up on her. "What?"

"We're going to pass you off as Coots's daughter. The story we'll give them is that you're a water hydraulics specialist learning the trade. Naturally, because that's my field, you'll be with me at all times. That way, the Bedouins are less likely to bother you. If I were you, I wouldn't wear any makeup, either. I'd try to look as much like a man as possible. Don't draw their attention if you can help it and whatever you do, don't wander away from our crew."

It sounded like someone's idea of a joke to her. But she could sense Sam's genuine concern. Rubbing her face, she muttered, "How in the hell do I get myself into such trouble?"

Sam shrugged. "Honey, I think you've been in and out of trouble all your life. There's a part of you that likes this adventure we're going on. There's another part that wants to be home right now in a nice bubble bath."

Kelly nodded. "You're right on both counts. But this is even a little farfetched for me. Just the same, I've got to prove that I'm willing to do whatever it takes to solve this problem with our pipe. I need to be there, Sam."

He grimaced. "I know, it's a matter of integrity and pride. Come here. Lie in my lap and stretch out. You might as well try to get some sleep. It's going to be a long flight."

She looked up at him, her heart beating more rapidly. "What about you? Aren't you tired?"

"Not yet. Come on, you first. I'll wake you up halfway through the flight and then you can be my pillow. Fair enough?"

Nodding, she capitulated without another word. Lying on her side, she allowed Sam to gather her into his arms. The roughness of the coveralls against her cheek, the drumming of his heart next to her ear served as a tranquilizer to her. The turbo-prop engines throbbed and the vibration of the aircraft soothed her. But it was Sam's arms around her that made her feel protected and she nuzzled more deeply into his arms like a lost child.

You're a beautiful fairy tale princess, Sam thought. But if you knew of my physical hunger for you, you would run from me like a wild mustang. Sam supported her body with his right arm. Bringing up his left hand, he gently moved several strands of her silken hair away from her cheek. She was childlike in some ways—trusting, vulnerable. And yet, she was all woman. His kind of woman. His eyes darkened as he drank in her form. He wanted to make love with her, touch that willful spirit that made her eyes shine like rare emerald fire and make her his own. She could be his—with a gentle hand and plenty of patience.

Patience, Tyler, he warned himself. But where they were going, time would be at a premium. A cold feeling crept up his spine and Sam automatically placed his left arm around Kelly. He sensed trouble. He remembered his tours in Nam and that same cold feeling snaking up his back to warn him of forthcoming danger. He glanced down at Kelly's blissful features. There was danger. Someone could be killed. Dear God, don't let it be Kelly. Give us a chance to know one another. Don't tear away this chance . . . please . . . But the strange, fluttering sensation in his chest wouldn't be stilled.

6

·⊙⊙⊙⊙⊙⊙⊙⊙⊙·

The bloody sunrise rose silently across the Rub al Khali Desert. Kelly stood watching the sun, transfixed by the crimson color that heralded dawn. She stood next to the fourth member of the team, Pat Crossley, an H2S expert and diesel mechanic. They had all seen the blowout almost two hundred miles in advance of landing. The orange and red flames roared four hundred feet into the air.

The cargo plane had landed on a hard dirt strip near some Bedouin tents. As the plane landed, it sent the herds of goats, sheep and camels scattering like leaves before the wind. They stepped out of the plane to a scene where pandemonium reigned.

Special flatbeds arrived and the huge skids in the plane were transferred to the trucks. Kelly watched as the Blanchard piperack skids were placed on a second truck. The extra pipe brought from another company remained on the ground. She walked over to where Boots was talking with someone dressed in a long, white woolen robe, inwardly wondering how anyone could stand the heat dressed like that. Even at six A.M., Kelly could feel sweat trickling down between her breasts and soaking into her lacy bra. She came to a halt, waiting for Boots to finish. Curiosity got the better of her and she stole a look up at the tall, swarthy Bedouin. Shock went through her as his black eyes bored into hers. She quickly lowered her gaze and stepped behind Boots.

"Look," Boots said in an exasperated tone, "you tell Sheik Hassad to get the crew of that gas rig back on site. We're gonna need some manpower. You understand? Also, we need bulldozers. At least three of them. And two backhoes. We radioed ahead. He said they'd be here."

The Arab shifted his piercing gaze from Kelly back to Boots. "Yes, yes. My master has followed your instructions. Everything is in readiness at the well. Come, come, we must hurry."

Boots nodded. "Give the keys of the trucks to our men. We'll drive."

"Yes, yes. Of course." The man bowed, took another keen look at Kelly and then turned, shouting a flurry of orders to his contingent of men.

Boots turned to her. "You ride with Sam. He told you about being Coots's daughter?"

"Yes. Boots, what about that other pipe? Aren't you taking it along?"

"Love to, honey, but we ain't got the room. We'll send a truck back for it." He put an arm around her waist. "Now come on. We got a show to get on the road. Sam's driving that piperack truck. Go keep him company."

It was a strange and hostile environment. Kelly said little as she rode with Sam, keeping her eyes and ears open. There was hardly a road to be followed as they drove through the torturous heat. The sheik's emissary led the way in a battered olive green jeep. Kelly glanced over at Sam. "The head honcho of the Arab contingent almost looks like he's a predatory bird ready to take off with his robes flying around him."

Sam mustered a tired smile. When it had come his turn to sleep he had found it damn near impossible. Lying on her long, beautifully shaped thighs, he had been unable to sleep for a long while. He could feel the yielding softness of her legs beneath him. He had yearned to turn on his shoulder, wrap his arms around her waist and bury his head in the soft warmth of her body.

Kelly had awakened him an hour before landing. A soft, almost maternal smile had touched her lips as he looked up at her. It would have been so easy to reach up and kiss those parted, inviting lips. . . .

"I guess it would look like that to someone who's never been over here before," he conceded. And then his voice took on a deeper tone. "I noticed that he was staring at you when you were with Boots earlier. Did he say anything?"

"No." She automatically checked to make sure her hair was tucked snugly beneath the white construction hat.

"Good. Listen, when we get there, stick close. There's going to be a helluva lot of confusion at first until we can get the government people settled down and get the sheik's men organized. The first hour or so is spent just calming the owners of any blowout." He grinned slightly, noting the clear emerald color of her guileless eyes. "You look like an eighteen-year-old, Kelly Blanchard. Freckles and all."

Kelly groaned. "No makeup! I feel absolutely naked!"

"But you look absolutely beautiful," Sam murmured fervently. Her lips were a natural cherry color. And her wide, childlike eyes made his heart blossom with a feeling he thought had died years before. "You're a witch, you know that," he said above the roar of the truck.

She laughed shyly. "Me? A witch? I've been called a few names, but never a witch."

"You're a good witch, though. A caster of spells on men like me who like redheads. I hope for your sake you don't have anybody special back home, Kelly Blanchard."

She colored prettily. "Sam Tyler!"

He grinned. "You look so pretty right now, I don't know if you'd be safer with the Arabs or me."

It was a magical moment. She had felt the magic before when she snuggled into his arms on the plane. And now, she felt it again. "I'll take you anytime," she vowed.

His eyes darkened. "You sure?" he asked huskily.

Kelly swallowed and her heart pounded unrelentingly in her breast. "Very sure."

"Okay . . . I'll hold you to that promise, my redhaired witch."

There was no time for further talk between them once they arrived at the blowout. Kelly's eyes widened, her gaze following the billowing flames roaring skyward. The noise was thunderous and talking was impossible.

"We're in luck," Sam shouted, grinding the flatbed to a halt.

"How?"

"That flame is nearly perfect. You want it to look like a candle flame. That means there's very little debris near the base of the pipe where the gas is coming out of the ground. Great."

The heat was stifling as she followed him across the baking sands to where the members of Boots and Coots were gathering. Already, Kelly felt the coveralls she wore being soaked with her own sweat. The roaring of the inferno was beyond belief, shattering the normal desert silence with the sound of an uncontrolled freight train hurtling downhill at ninety miles an hour. Everywhere she looked, Kelly saw blackened, twisted metal girders that had once been part of the drilling tower. It was an awesome sight and it sent fear through her. How could they cap that roaring monster?

In the midst of the semi-circle of gathering men, Kelly saw a tall, proud figure in cream colored wool robes. It was the sheik. Sticking close to Sam, she walked over to join the group.

Coots was standing in the center of the group talking, and almost immediately the agitated sheik and government officials began calming down. The first step was clearing the mangled debris away from the wellhead. In no time, the sheik's men were mounted on the bulldozers. Boots ordered them down off the machinery. Much had yet to be done before they could actually begin to clear the debris away. More than once the sheik's dark, piercing eyes lingered on Kelly. She remained silent, her arm against Sam's, wishing she could hide. Kelly didn't like the sheik, his arrogant gestures, his imperial stance or the guttural orders he gave Boots and Coots.

After a plan was agreed upon, Sam took her by the

arm and pulled her away from the group. "Come on, we'll begin laying pipe from the well to the blowout site."

Once in the truck, Sam handed her a canteen filled with water. Sweat trickled down his face as he watched her drink. "Not too much, Kelly." He dug out a packet of salt tablets and placed them in her hand. "Take a couple of these every few hours when you drink the water. Heat exhaustion is a fact of life out here," he warned. "And chances are, you've never encountered this kind of heat before."

"Never," Kelly agreed, giving him the canteen. "I wonder how hot it is now?"

"Probably around ninety. It'll get up to a hundred and fifteen or twenty by this afternoon," he growled.

"You're kidding me! How can anyone work in that kind of heat?"

He closed the canteen, placing it back on the seat. "We do. But not you. We're lucky on this fire. We've got a water well and the porta-camp will be erected by this evening. It's our home until we cap this blowout. The porta-camp is a modular type structure that's air conditioned. When you start feeling fatigued, get yourself inside."

It was nightfall before the porta-camp was completely erected. Kelly was amazed to find that the small corrugated shacks were surprisingly cool. The first shack would house a cooking and eating area. The other two contained cots and the barest of essentials. Electricity was provided by portable generators. The flooring consisted of heavy plywood.

Disappointment registered on Kelly's face. The clankety-clank of a straining air conditioner filled the inside of the supply shack. A light film of sand had already settled on everything and she wrinkled her nose, running her finger over a small desk which held the drilling logs. She removed her hard hat, glad she had pinned her hair high on her head. Although the air conditioning was set at maximum, it was probably eighty degrees inside. Well, she'd just have to get used to sweating whether she liked it or not. Right now, at Boots's request, she was logging in the boxes and cartons of food and other supplies. When the last box was checked off the manifest, Kelly signed the top sheet and handed it to the waiting truck driver. He bowed and murmured his thanks in Arabic and Kelly mumbled "Thank you" in English.

It was nearly nine P.M. when Kelly tiredly made her rounds with the five-gallon jug of water for the men of Boots and Coots. Excavation of debris surrounding the outer perimeter of the blowout was nearly complete. Large water monitor nozzles had been erected and were protected by huge corrugated galvanized shields. The nozzles were then positioned within two hundred feet of the roaring inferno. Every breath she took made her lungs feel as if they were on fire. How she wanted to crawl back to the safety of those shacks! Doggedly, Kelly slogged through the sand, walking toward Boots. Her feet felt as if they were being burned up. Boots's darkly bronzed face lit up with a smile when he saw her approaching. Although darkness had curtained the desert, around the blowout it was like daylight.

"You're a doll, honey," Boots said, taking the water and drinking from the tin cup. "Thanks."

Colly glanced over at her. "How you doing, Kelly? Hot enough for ya?"

She managed a grin. "Just a little. I feel like a fried egg in a skillet."

Boots nodded, giving Colly the water jug and cup. "You just make damn sure you take care of yourself. You ain't used to this kind of heat. I've seen more than one man keel over with heat exhaustion." He motioned toward a helicopter that had landed an hour earlier. "Know what that's for?"

Kelly shook her head.

"It's for medical emergency airlift. If anyone gets injured, he'll be flown to Abu Dhabi which has the nearest hospital. I don't want to have to use that damn thing on this call."

She agreed. Taking the jug, she trudged back to the battered white pickup she was using to make the rounds. Just as she reached for the door handle, a dark arm snaked out from behind her.

Momentarily stunned, Kelly froze. The long fingers wrapped around her waist, forcing her to turn around. The curious gaze of the sheik met her startled eyes. A catlike smile lit his angular face as he stared down at her.

Kelly's heart thudded with sudden fear. She jerked her wrist free. "Get your hands off me!" Escape! She had to escape!

The sheik lifted both hands. "Ah, an American rose with thorns, no doubt. Hamid was telling me there was a beautiful woman on the team." His smile deepened, sending a shiver of dread through her. "He was not wrong."

"Well," she croaked, her throat tight with fear, "you're right on one account. I'm no American rose, but I damn sure have thorns. Now please let me get into the truck. I've got work to do!"

He tilted his head, the smile fading from his thin mouth. "You should be trained to be quiet, woman."

A new wave of fear engulfed Kelly. The words had slid from his mouth like an unsheathed dagger. For an instant, she thought he was going to raise his hand to slap her. Out of instinct, she had tensed, bringing her arm close to her body to ward off the blow.

A glitter of animal savagery flickered in his eyes. "Still," he murmured, "you are desirable. Headstrong but not untamable."

Anger mixed with fear inside her.

"Trouble, Kelly?"

Sam's voice! She wanted to cry with relief as she saw him approaching.

"Just a little," she managed, leaning heavily against the truck door.

The sheik turned, silently appraising the man who stood before him like a prizefighter. "She is your woman?" he asked.

Sam nodded. "That's right, she's mine," he growled softly.

The sheik allowed a hint of a smile. "You ought to teach her better manners, then. If one of my wives spoke to me like that, I would cut off the tip of her tongue."

Kelly blanched. The Bedouin was serious! Wide-eyed, she sought Sam's gaze. But Sam's eyes were locked with the sheik's.

"Where I come from, we like our women to speak up."

"She needs taming."

"No one tames her. If she spoke harshly to you, then you had it coming."

"No woman dares speak to me in that tone."

Sam allowed a hint of a smile to pull at one corner of his mouth. He deliberately reached out, pulling Kelly to his side, his arm wrapped protectively around her shoulders. "What happened, Kelly?" he asked, meeting her fearful gaze.

Quickly, she told Sam, her voice scratchy as the sheik continued to glare down at her. Sam's face hardened as he turned toward the man.

"You were told she's Coots Matthews' daughter. No one bothers her on this site."

The sheik gave an eloquent shrug of his shoulders. "She is merely a woman. Nothing more."

"It had better mean something more than that," Sam warned. "I don't think your government would be too happy if we pulled out because you harassed one of our employees. And she does work for the company in an official capacity."

The Bedouin's eyes showed disbelief. "You would leave simply because I touched this woman?" A slow smile twisted his lips. "Warriors kill over honorable circumstances." He glared at Kelly. "She is not worth shedding blood over," he sneered.

"Your instructions were to provide us with adequate security and to leave this woman alone," Sam grated. "Our customs differ. If you want us to cap this well, you place your attentions elsewhere."

Kelly's anger overrode her fear. She felt Sam's fingers tighten in warning on her shoulder and she swallowed her retort. The sheik continued to look her up and down as if she were a piece of marketable meat. She trembled with rage.

He gave Sam a measuring look. "She is your wife?"

"No."

"Ahh, then your slave?"

"Now look here—" Kelly objected heatedly.

"Shut up, Kelly."

"That is more like it," the sheik praised, directing all his attention to Sam. "The color of her hair matches her temper. If she is not your wife, then I will make you an offer, Mr. Tyler," he continued, ignoring Kelly completely, as if she didn't exist. "I have one of the finest racing camel herds on the Rub al Khali. I will give you ten of my best camels for her."

Kelly gasped, jerking free of Sam's arm and positioning herself between both men. "Now you listen to me, you damn chauvinist—"

Sam growled an epithet and yanked open the truck door. "Dammit," he hissed, "get in that truck and get back to the camp! Now."

She gave Sam a shaken look, chilled by his sudden change. His face was stony, his eyes nearly black as he slammed the door. Kelly glared one last time at the sheik, both pleased and terrified that the Bedouin's face was livid with rage. Without a word, she started up the truck and drove off, leaving the two men to face one another.

Sam turned slowly to the sheik. Fear clashed with anger inside him. Kelly had done more damage than she could ever realize. The Bedouin was trembling. No woman could speak to a man, according to their customs, like she had, and get away without punishment. And Sam had been to these parts enough times to realize her gaffe was going to create problems. "Look," he ground out, "she is not for sale at *any* price. She is Coots's daughter. She is my woman."

Hassad's eyes became slits as he regarded the American. "You are in my country," he reminded him in a steely voice. "Our women are not allowed into such areas as this. If you take the responsibility of bringing that devil with red hair here, then she must behave properly or be punished."

"There will be no punishment. You want that well capped? What if we leave? What will your government think of your actions? It wouldn't look good if trouble over a woman is the cause of this well not being put out."

Hassad drew himself erect, his black eyes blazing with the awful light of righteous anger. "She has insulted me. The law forbids me to allow her to go unpunished."

"I'll punish her myself," Sam gritted out. At that instant, he wanted to wrap his hands around Kelly's slender white throat and throttle her.

"I will extract my own form of justice," Hassad snarled.

Sam tensed. "Don't threaten me."

The sheik appraised him. "It was a woman who insulted me, not you. She will answer to me. You and I have no quarrel."

Sam reached out, his fingers sinking deeply into the sheik's forearm. "Now look," he rasped, "drop the idea of punishing her. She is my property and I'll deal with her in my own way. Understand?"

Hassad jerked his arm away. "I understand perfectly." He spun around and walked toward his jeep. The entire episode was unresolved.

"Damn!" Tyler cursed, walking in the direction of the camp. He had been worried about guerrilla activity before. Now Kelly had managed to stir up the local sheik and bruise his ego. Clenching and unclenching his dirty fists, he trudged toward the quarters to confront her.

He found her in the kitchen shack, preparing coffee. She turned toward him when he entered. Her eyes were ablaze with anger. Wearily, he pulled the white construction hat off his head and dropped it on the makeshift table between them. Her gaze clashed with his.

"What the hell did you think you were doing out there?" she demanded hotly. "You had no business—"

"Calm down, Kelly."

She set the coffeepot down on the plywood surface with a loud bang. "Calm down? When that bastard made me out to be nothing more than a piece of meat to be sold! Come off it, Sam! How can he say such things?"

He put up his hand. Damn, she was a hellion when she got her back up. "Because we're in his country," he roared back. "Now sit down here and talk with me. I don't want to start a screaming match." His blue eyes met her glare. "Come on," he coaxed, "sit down here with me. This is far more serious than you realize."

Her shoulders slumped and suddenly she was exhausted. "Okay," she agreed. "I'm sorry I started screaming at you. It wasn't your fault."

"If I had been in your shoes, I'd probably have decked him," Sam confided.

Kelly sat down dejectedly. "I was minding my own business, Sam. Can't I even give water to our men without seeming to be a liberated female to these Bedouins?"

He rubbed his face tiredly. "No. But it doesn't matter." He gripped her hand. "Look, you insulted Hassad in the worst possible manner. Women never talk directly to their men over here, much less curse at them. He's angry and he wants revenge."

"What kind of revenge?" she asked slowly, her heart beginning to pound.

Sam released her hand. "Hell, I don't know. I told him

if he didn't leave you alone, we'd leave his damn gas well uncapped and go home."

She blinked. "You would?"

"Absolutely. Coots made it clear to the government officials that you were to be treated as a member of our team or else. Above all, Kelly, you're going to have to watch what you say. I know it isn't fair, but who said everything in life was fair?"

His words sobered her. "You're right . . . Thank God you came when you did. I was so frightened. He meant business. . . ." Her voice became inaudible.

"The incident may blow over, providing you make yourself scarce." He allowed himself a small grin. "And as long as you don't mind being known as my woman around the site."

She gazed into his eyes, feeling incredibly happy at his nearness. "I don't mind at all," she assured him fervently. Shakily, she buried her face in her hands. "Everything's so alien, Sam," she said in a muffled voice. "It's horrible! The heat's bad enough but the Bedouins' attitude toward women is . . . is . . ."

In one motion, Sam was on his feet and around the table, pulling her into his arms. His large hands spanned her slender waist and he drew her against him. "Come here," he ordered huskily. "It'll be all right. You're just tired and it's been one hell of a long day."

Kelly shuddered, finding solace against him. She was wildly aware of his maleness, of his hand on her waist, drawing her daringly to his hips. Her pulse throbbed, but this time it wasn't out of fear. It was out of incredible longing. She slid her hands across his massive chest, encircling his neck with her arms. He groaned and his grip tightened convulsively around her straining body.

"Kelly . . ." he whispered. She was so spirited, so willing, so feminine. Capturing her chin with his callused hand, he tilted her head up to meet his descending mouth. He grazed her lips, glorying in the pliancy of her flesh beneath his own. He felt her shudder and pressed his mouth more insistently on hers. Her lips parted at his demand. He heard her moan softly as he deepened his exploration of her honied depths. Her breathing became chaotic; her nipples hardened beneath the material of her coveralls. Slowly, he left her willing lips and stared darkly into her open eyes.

He hadn't meant to kiss her. But it had seemed so right. So . . . he groped for explanations but none would come. His body throbbed with hunger for her. His gaze dropped back to her mouth, now wet and pouty from his kiss. He felt instant regret. He hadn't meant to hurt her with the bruising kiss but they had come together like fire and oil, igniting yearnings he had never experienced before. He gently traced the outline of her jaw.

"You're one hell of a woman," he murmured gruffly, his voice unsteady.

Kelly inhaled deeply. She was trembling to the core of her being. There was no longer any doubt in her mind or heart that she was Sam Tyler's woman. That one kiss had been savage but it had claimed her heart, body and soul for him. Weakly, she leaned against his arms. "I could say similar things about you," she added breathlessly. Her whole body craved further contact with Sam. She lifted her auburn lashes, meeting his azure gaze. "Oh, Sam . . ." she whispered faintly. Her body sang in triumph. She saw the beginning of a tender smile on his mouth as he leaned down.

This time, his kiss was infinitely gentle, searching,

cajoling her to participate in their mutual discovery of one another. She drank deeply of his mouth. Their tongues entwined, stroking and teasing one another. It was a kiss celebrating the joy they found in one another, a joy that had been a long time in coming, but was all the more potent for the wait.

Sam drew away, drinking in her flushed features. Her green eyes were seductive looking, her lips parted. He reluctantly put her at arm's length, a thoughtful smile pulling at one corner of his mouth.

His fingers tightened momentarily around her torso. It would be easy to slide his hands up her ribcage and caress those small, erect breasts. . . . He ignored his selfish desire. One look at her blissful features and he knew that she was his. It was a matter of time and patience, he told himself severely. A woman like Kelly Blanchard would not allow herself to be pushed into anything. His blue eyes were rueful. "I think I'd better let you sit down before you fall down."

Kelly mutely agreed, her knees feeling like jelly. She couldn't trust her voice.

"Did you put any coffee in that percolator while you were rummaging around in here?" he asked, breaking the spell that bound them.

"No." Her voice was wispy. She saw Sam smile down at her.

"You okay?" he murmured, helping her to a chair.

"Give me five minutes and I'll let you know."

"You look beautiful to me," he teased, reaching over and picking up the coffeepot.

A tender smile played across her lips as she watched him make coffee. The heat was stifling in the trailer, but she was unaware of it. All her attention was centered on the man working quietly in the crowded space. Despite his large hands, he made even delicate work look easy. He proceeded to discuss the digging of the three huge earthen pits that would soon be lined with plastic and filled with the nearby well water.

Minutes later Kelly held the cup of coffee between her hands, sipping the hot liquid.

"As soon as we get those pits filled, we'll find out how well the pipe will stand up," he went on, sitting down across from her. "I intend to gradually increase the pressure of the water flowing through those pipes to the monitors."

Kelly tried to focus on the business at hand. She ran the fingers of one hand through her hair in a nervous gesture. She was behaving like a love-starved woman. Well, wasn't she? How many years ago had Todd stopped loving her? *I've got to get hold of myself,* she thought, feeling panic. *Could any man have made her feel this way? Or only Sam Tyler?*

By ten P.M. they began clearing the debris away from the base of the destroyed rig. Kelly joined Sam, watching as a sixty-foot-long crane with a huge hook assembly on one end was attached to an athey wagon. It was then pushed along the scorched desert floor toward the blazing fire storm. Coots Matthews was directing the whole operation with hand signals.

Sam had jury rigged three unmanned monitors so that thousands of gallons of water spewed out in a fog pattern upon the fire. The water cooled the area from twenty-five hundred degrees to five hundred degrees, allowing the athey wagons close enough to pick up the debris. The heat was intense near the gas well. The hissing of steam mingled with the roar of the gas being released from the bowels of the earth. Kelly stood near a flatbed, arms folded against her breast as she watched Sam climb up on one bulldozer.

The athey wagon, a miniature bulldozer without a cab, was unmanned and it took the brunt of heat from the blowout. Worriedly, Kelly watched as Sam urged the operator of the bulldozer closer and closer to the fire. The roar of the holocaust forced everyone to wear earplugs. She was amazed at the multitude of hand signals the team members flashed back and forth to one another to coordinate the gigantic effort.

The effects of jet lag and the stress of the day were taking their toll on Kelly. Finally, after watching the operation for more than an hour, she turned in. The shacks had little more in the way of bedding than cotton mats on which to sleep. She had been assigned a small room in the rear where the air conditioner was positioned. Sam would take no argument from her, telling her she needed the coolest room because she was not used to the extreme temperature. Reluctantly, Kelly agreed. The low-watt bulb in the bathroom provided enough light for her to wash. The water was tepid as she scrubbed herself clean.

Feeling almost human, she slipped into a light cotton nightgown of pale pink and padded softly to her room. Kelly stared at the door. Should she leave it ajar so that the coolness of the air conditioning would continue to spread throughout the entire area? Sam had told her in no uncertain terms to lock the door. Still, she felt guilty. She didn't want to rob the men of what little coolness was available. Images of their sweaty, strained faces danced before her tired eyes. To hell with it, she decided wearily, I'm leaving it open.

Curling up on the thick mat, Kelly quickly fell into a deep slumber. Outside the small window the yellow and orange glow created an eerie light. But even the light and the freight-train roar of the blowout didn't prevent Kelly from falling asleep.

7

Shadowy figures crept like ghosts through the quiet shack. Needle in hand, one of them stole into the last bedroom. Deftly, he slid the hypo into the sleeping woman's thigh. A brief moan came from her as she roused incoherently from sleep, her hand moving instinctively to her leg. He crouched down on his haunches, waiting . . . watching. A smile edged his lips. It was too late for her to help herself. Within thirty seconds the white-skinned woman with the fiery red hair would slide into a heavily drugged state. Satisfied, he stood, turned and motioned his accomplices to join him. Within moments they had wrapped her unconscious body in a dark wool burnoose and slid a large burlap bag over her head and shoulders. At a quick nod from the leader, one of the men hoisted her easily upon his thickly muscled shoulder, and they hurried out of the shack.

* * *

Sam wearily entered the porta-camp, throwing his dirty hard hat on the table. Boots, Coots and Colly followed closely behind. It was almost three A.M. and exhaustion showed on every man's face. Sam glanced down the hall toward the sleeping quarters. He frowned. Why the hell was Kelly's door open? Cursing under his breath, he walked toward it. Damn her. He had told her to lock it. Moving quietly, he gripped the doorknob and pushed it back just enough to check on her. His eyes adjusted quickly to the darkness. Scowling, he stared down at the empty pallet in the corner.

"Kelly?" he called, stepping inside. His heart began a slow pound as he approached the sleeping mat. Kneeling down, he touched it, his throat constricting. It was cool to his hand. Glancing around, he stood up. Maybe she was in another room. . . . Quickly, he checked the other two.

"Boots, Coots," Sam called, returning to the dining room area.

Boots wearily raised his blond head. "Yeah?"

Sam's eyes were dark with fear. "Kelly. She isn't here."

Coots looked up scowling. "What are you talking about?"

Fear ate at Sam. "Maybe she's in the other shack. I'm going over to check."

He came back after five minutes, his face hardened. "She's gone," Sam said.

Boots looked at his partner. "This smells," he growled, rising.

"It's the sheik," Sam hissed.

"What are you talking about?" Boots demanded, his face betraying his agitation.

"Kelly had a run-in with Sheik Hassad earlier today. He wanted to punish her for showing him disrespect. I told him to keep his hands off her, that Kelly was my woman." Sam angrily ran his fingers through his damp hair. "Damn it, anyway!"

Coots's mouth turned into a grim line. "We'd better move fast on this one. White slavery is damned profitable over here." He cast a look over at Sam. "I wonder if Hassad wants Kelly for himself or if he's gonna sell her outright."

Tyler released a string of oaths. "Where's his camp? I'll take a truck out there right now."

Boots gripped Sam's arm. "He's stupider than I thought. He was told earlier she was Coots's daughter. Is he out of his mind?"

Sam jerked one of the metal suitcases from beneath the bench, quickly unlocking it with the proper combination. Inside were holsters and .357 magnum pistols. Grabbing one, he buckled it around his waist. "Coots, I think you'd better come with me since Kelly is supposed to be your daughter."

"You going to confront him now?" Boots asked.

Sam's eyes flashed with anger and fear. "Hell yes. If he's thinking of shipping Kelly out of the country, I don't want to give him a head start." He jerked a look over at Coots. "You coming?"

"Yeah, you bet. Hand me that other pistol," he ordered.

"What about this well?" Boots asked.

Sam turned at the door. "You tell the government, if

we don't get their cooperation in this matter, we'll let it burn until doomsday."

Boots agreed. "Look, I'll grab the head honcho right now and find out where Hassad's camp is located. I'll continue to coordinate from this end. Take one of the portable radios. That way, we'll be in contact."

Sam nodded, picking up the radio he normally carried in his belt. "Good idea," he agreed.

Kelly moaned, and a shaft of pain shot through her head. She rolled listlessly onto her back. Her mouth felt like it was filled with cottonballs and her throat was dry for lack of water. Her eyelids felt as if a hundred tons of weight had been placed upon them. She forced them open. Where was she? Sounds, different sounds from the ones at the blowout, drifted into her consciousness. The soft whinny of nearby horses mingled with the muted bleating of goats or sheep. Pain forced her to lie still. Groaning, Kelly held her head and curled up into a fetal position.

She slept again to escape the pain. The second time she awoke, reality returned almost immediately. She sat up and her hair tumbled across her shoulders and down the front of her cotton nightgown. Her lips were chapped and dry. She gazed around. Was she in a tent? The walls around her were of heavy canvaslike material, and a rug was on the ground beneath her. A man holding a rifle in his arms at the only entrance to her room drew her attention. Fear began to eat away at her composure. Frowning, Kelly touched her thigh. Just a slight amount of pressure caused pain. Pulling up the gown, she saw a huge black and blue bruise around what appeared to be an insect bite. Trying to swallow against the fear, Kelly struggled to her knees.

"Hey!" she croaked. "Hey! Where am I?"

The guard turned, giving her a steady but unreadable look. Another similarly clothed and armed guard came to the entrance and they conversed about her in an unintelligible language.

Kelly forced herself to stand but she was unsteady. She placed a hand on her forehead, trying to relieve the sudden pain that standing up had produced. "Dammit," she growled, forcing one foot ahead of the other. The guard turned, his gaze drilling into her. Kelly halted.

"What's going on here? Where's Coots Matthews? I want to see Sam Tyler!"

The guard gave her a blank look. Around his waist he wore a scimitar as long as a man's arm. Kelly decided to retreat to the center of the room. Her mind was spongy. Why couldn't she think straight? After carefully sitting down, Kelly cradled her aching head. Something was desperately wrong. Where was Sam? What was that horrid bruise on her leg? Nothing made sense. . . .

"Ahh, I see my American rose with thorns has awakened," a voice growled.

Kelly jerked her head up. A gasp escaped her as she recognized Sheik Hassad. He gave her a perfunctory smile as he entered the room.

One part of her wanted to be as far away from him as possible. But another part of her said, hold your ground. He'll hunt you down if you show fear or cowardice. She mustered what little courage she had left and thrust out her jaw, her green eyes blazing.

"Just what is going on? Where am I? And how did I get here?"

Hassad folded his long hands together. "Are you always a rose with thorns? I think I shall call you Thorn from now on, to remind me that you have a caustic tongue."

She clenched her teeth. "You're not making sense!"

Hassad smiled broadly, looking like a wolf who had effectively cornered his prey. He leaned down and stroked her fiery red-gold hair. She jerked away from him and scrambled to her feet, weaving drunkenly from the effects of the drug.

Hassad straightened, his eyes glittering with a terrible light. "Even a rose with thorns must learn when to be still. You are mine now," he said, his voice deepening with chilling authority. He watched her large green eyes widen incredulously. "I have chosen you as the newest member of my harem. Henceforth, you will be called Thorn." His smile disappeared. "And if you do not curb yourself, woman, I will take great delight in ridding you of your tongue myself."

Kelly stared in disbelief and horror. This couldn't be happening! This was almost the twenty-first century! She was an American! "You kidnapped me!" she yelled. "Against my wishes. You can't do that and get away with it! Tyler will kill you when he finds out what you've done. I'm his woman. Not yours!"

Hassad gave her a suave smile. "I will make you mine tonight. My five wives will prepare and anoint you, Thorn. If you do not cooperate, I shall personally break your fiery spirit once and for all."

Kelly stared at him in total shock. He left as quietly as he had come. With a small cry, she sank to her knees, fighting against the sobs that threatened to tear from her throat. Oh, God! Sam, she screamed in her mind and heart, Sam, where are you? I can't . . . I won't submit to that horrid monster! I won't!

She sat cross-legged, forcing herself to think clearly. She had to get control of her emotions. She had to accept the fact that she was kidnapped. Why hadn't she paid attention to Sam's warning to lock the bedroom door? A hundred recriminations drove her more deeply into gloom.

As her head cleared, Kelly formed a plan. She ate the food given to her and drank deeply of the tepid water from the goatskin bag. Sam had to be hunting for her. He must! Desperation entwined with fear. She tied her thick mass of hair into a ponytail and searched the room for clothing. A small ornate chest yielded various pieces of masculine attire. She discovered a pair of men's pants and slipped them on beneath the nightgown. She had heard the whinny of horses. No stranger to riding, Kelly grimly decided to try to escape by horseback. The guard slowly walked back and forth in front of the open entrance.

Judging from the slant of the sun beneath the tent tarp, Kelly guessed it must be near three in the afternoon. The bottom flap of the tent was not that carefully staked down. There was just enough room for her to slip beneath the edge of it. Fear closed her throat as she counted the seconds until the guard passed. She had no idea where Hassad's camp was located or which direction to go. The only guide might possibly be the blowout. How far could they have taken her in one night? The flame from the well would guide her! She trembled visibly, fear making her heart pound wildly. The choice was either to try to escape now or be raped tonight. She shivered, her skin crawling as she thought of Hassad's talonlike fingers on her body. No!

Now! She dropped to the floor, squeezing out from beneath the tent. The sunlight made her squint. Without shoes, the soles of her feet were burned by the sand, but she was oblivious to the pain. To her left stood at least eight Arabian horses tied to a long rope. All were saddled. Sprinting through the sand, Kelly closed the distance between her and the animals. A shout in Arabic suddenly erupted behind her. She flinched and continued running.

The horse closest to her jumped sideways as she lunged for the reins. More screams and curses rent the air. In seconds, she was mounted and kicking the horse. The wind tore at her as she yelled at the animal, taking the leather reins and slashing them downward along the animal's shoulders. She looked back. Horror overrode her triumph. At least five men were mounting in pursuit!

Grimly, Kelly glanced around. There! To the east lay the blowout. She guided the white mare in that direction. The horse fairly skimmed the undulating sand dunes. Her hair, once bound, had come undone, the fiery red cascade flying across her shoulders. The horse ran tirelessly. Kelly had expected that any animal running in the stifling heat would collapse within the first ten minutes. But it wasn't so. The mare's nostrils flared blood red, but it took each dune with seeming ease. And at each rise, Kelly glanced back over her shoulder to find that the five men pursuing her were no closer than before. She saw them brandishing swords and two of them held rifles high above their heads. Would they fire on her? Would they try to hit her horse to halt her escape? Fear forced her to urge the horse even faster.

Time melted into the inferno around her. Very soon she was feeling lightheaded. Whether it was a drug reaction or the effects of the horrible sun beating down upon her unprotected head and body, she had no idea. The white mare had broken out in a sweat. Kelly gripped at the saddle, which had no horn. She willed herself to stay alert, forced herself to move in unison with the galloping horse. If she fell off . . . if she fainted . . . No! She would rather die first than go back into that bastard's harem! Heat waves hung like heavy shimmering curtains in all directions as Kelly crossed the reflective white sands. Her arms were red with sunburn in no time, her head ached fiercely and she felt the cotton nightgown clinging to her upper body, soaked with perspiration.

Kelly rode directly toward the blowout. She had lost track of time, knowing only that her five pursuers were slowly gaining on her now. It was a silent, deadly battle and she clung to the saddle, her legs rubbed raw because she had lost the rhythm of the mare beneath her. Blackness started to edge Kelly's vision and she screamed. The mare increased her pace momentarily, startled. Anything to stay conscious! The heat was eating her alive. She felt faint, as if she were in an overheated oven that was ready to explode. Her mouth and throat were parched. Her eyeballs felt baked. Follow the flame, she shouted to herself. The flame! Have to get to Sam. Oh Sam, I love you! I love you! God, give me a chance to tell you that. Just let me get back! And the litany continued for another hour while she stubbornly held on to the mare. The exhausted animal had slowed now to a trot.

One long, curving sand dune loomed above them. The blowout didn't seem any closer. Kelly called to the mare, digging her heels weakly into the horse's heaving, foam-flecked flanks. Her five pursuers were inexorably closing the distance. It was only a matter of time. . . . The mare snorted and tensed her hindquarters. Sand flew in all directions beneath her hooves. Finally, with one more lunge, they crested the long, graceful sand dune.

Kelly fell forward, her hands slippery against the mare's wet mane. She barely caught herself. She drew on her last ounce of courage to hang on and fight back. Through sheer force of will, Kelly made herself sit upright as she rode the mare across the top of the dune. Her vision grayed as she looked toward the blowout. Wavering curtains of heat distorted everything. Was her mind playing tricks on her? Did she see a cloud of dust coming in her direction? Was it a white flatbed? A croaking sob tore from her throat. She had no strength left to turn and see how close her pursuers were. No strength. . . .

Dropping forward on the mare's neck, Kelly gripped the mane, barely able to hold on to the trotting horse. She heard the snort of horses closing in from behind her. They would soon be abreast of her . . . they would capture her. She had no tears left to cry. Sam! Oh, Sam, I love you. I did from the moment we met! Oh, God, we'll never know . . . I'm falling . . . falling . . . I love you so much! Can't hang on . . . can't . . .

Sam watched in horror as Kelly pitched over the head of the horse she was riding. No more than two hundred yards behind was the contingent of Bedouin horsemen in hot pursuit. Their rifles were raised as they spurred their mounts up toward where Kelly lay prostrate.

"Hurry!" he yelled at Coots. Hot, blistering wind hit Sam's face as he aimed the pistol out the window. There was no way they would take Kelly again! He squeezed the trigger. The shot cracked through the sweltering heat.

"They ain't gonna stop!" Coots yelled, pressing the accelerator to the floor. The truck bucked and lurched, its heavily treaded tires digging into the sand.

Sam's face was frozen in concentration. Sweat ran down his temples; his face glistened. His mouth compressed into a single line of fury. His eyes narrowed with angry intensity as he lowered the barrel of the pistol. His first shot had been in warning. This time . . .

Sam fired a second time. The leader on a bay horse had just crested the hill. The shot caught the horse in the chest. The animal screamed, knees buckling, and pitched off the rider.

They were closing in on Kelly! Just a few hundred more feet! Sam fired another shot above the Bedouins. He watched as the horseless rider scrambled to his feet. Another rider rode forward, hand outstretched to pull the first up behind him. The five Bedouins milled about in momentary confusion.

Coots slammed on the brakes and the truck sloughed to a stop. Sam leaped out of the truck with the pistol held in a threatening position. Coots grabbed another pistol and came around the front of the truck. Sam's heart thudded heavily in his chest as he gripped the pistol with both hands and lowered it at the Bedouins.

"Don't try it!" he shouted, focusing on the leader.

The armed Bedouins exchanged glances and then quickly turned and sped back down the large sand dune. Sam glared at them briefly before running the last few yards to where Kelly lay unmoving.

A small whimper issued from Kelly's throat. Coolness was spreading down her brow, across her cheeks to her parched, cracked lips. Water! Droplets were dribbled between her lips and she moaned as the water reached her raw, parched throat. Sounds, very far away, penetrated her semiconscious state.

"You're safe, honey. It's Sam. Just rest. Don't fight me. You're with me. We're going home . . ."

Sam's words rang like joyful music in her head. She must be dreaming! She had to be. Her body felt as if it were on fire. Slowly, like mismatched jigsaw puzzle pieces, the events of the past day and night came back to her. Kelly barely had the strength to lift her lashes. It was impossible. She was aware of men's voices, the growl of a truck engine laboring at high speed and jostling motion. Arms . . . strong arms were holding her. And a cool cloth was being held against her hot, burning flesh. She was dreaming. It was all a wishful dream. Her brows pulled downward and a weak cry rose in her throat. The sheik had recaptured her!

Sam grimly caught her flailing arms, holding Kelly tightly against his chest. She struggled only briefly in her semiconscious state. A soft mewing sound came from her and it tore his heart in pieces. Coots exchanged a worried look with him, saying nothing. He was driving the flatbed for all it was worth. The hot wind tore through the opened windows, sending Kelly's red hair into soft disarray. Sam's blue eyes were hard and shiny with tears as he held her tightly. Her skin was feverishly hot. She was burning up. He had worked on too many desert blowouts not to recognize that Kelly had suffered a sunstroke. And it could kill her if they couldn't get her body cooled down in time.

"Hurry," he growled to Coots.

8

Kelly awakened to the sounds of her own sobs. A warm, callused hand gently brushed the tears from her cheek and Kelly fought to become conscious.

"It's all right, honey," Sam soothed in a reassuring tone. He had been sitting or sleeping in the chair at Kelly's bedside for the last forty-eight hours. He glanced across the room at the doctor and nurse who had come in at his request.

Kelly moaned, reliving the horror of the kidnapping, fighting the last effects of the powerful tranquilizing drug that the Bedouins had given her.

"Sam . . ." she moaned.

"Right here, Kelly. It's all right. You're safe."

"Oh, Sam." With that she lapsed back into an unintelligible garble.

He took a damp, cool cloth and gently dabbed her

brow and cheeks. Anxiously, he watched as the doctor took her pulse and blood pressure. For the last two days Kelly's life had hung in the balance. He had first thought she had only suffered a serious sunstroke.

Instead, it was discovered in the emergency room that Kelly was also having an adverse drug reaction coupled with a drug overdose. Sam wearily rubbed his face with his free hand, as if to force back the deluge of emotions that threatened to break. He loved Kelly. That simple realization had torn his very soul apart as he watched the doctors fight for her life. And after forty-eight hours of being in a coma, she was finally regaining consciousness.

Sam continued to stroke her brow. He had found that she was more tranquil if he continued to talk to her and touch her during that hazy state between consciousness and unconsciousness. He shot a keen look at the doctor.

"What's happening?"

"She's coming out of the coma, Mr. Tyler." He allowed a brief smile. "She's going to make it. Remain with her if you want. The nurse will call me when she becomes more coherent."

The relief on Sam's face was obvious. He gazed down at Kelly, the hotness of tears stinging his burning eyes. His hand trembled slightly as he brushed it over her forehead.

"Thank God," he whispered unsteadily. He looked up at the doctor. "Thanks for pulling her through. . . ." He couldn't finish. Tears choked off the rest of his reply.

"Only give us half the credit, Mr. Tyler. It was her will to live that tipped the balance in our favor. I'll be back in about an hour."

Sam watched as they left and then returned his full

attention to Kelly. Her raving was becoming intelligible; the delirium was receding.

"I love you, Kelly Blanchard," he whispered thickly. Reaching over, he took her hand to reassure her as she broke through the last confines of the drugs.

Kelly stared in the mirror that the nurse had handed her. She carefully touched her face, which was still pink from sunburn. Had it only been a week since Sam and Coots had rescued her from Hassad's camp? Her heart beat more quickly when she recalled becoming conscious in Sam's arms on the way to the hospital. He had told her that they'd driven like madmen to the helicopter stationed at the blowout and then had flown the rest of the way to Abu Dhabi. And it had been Sam who was holding her hand when she finally awoke from the terrifying experience two days after that.

Kelly's eyes darkened. She would never forget Sam's face that evening. His eyes were red-rimmed and the growth of his beard made his features appear gaunt and shadowed. He had been crying. Somewhere in her half dream, half nightmare state, she had heard him calling her back, calling her to his side. Kelly lowered her lashes. Had she imagined him saying that he loved her? In a pensive gesture, she drew a brush the nurse had brought through her freshly washed hair. The reddish-gold strands were finally clean of sand and grit. She never forgot his parting kiss on her chapped, cracked lips, either. He had explained that he had to get back to the blowout. That in a week he would come and visit her again. Kelly closed her eyes, remembering her reaction. She had begun to cry. Great, tearing sobs. He had gathered her up in his arms with great tenderness, rocking her back and forth. His voice was a healing balm for her injured soul and gradually, she had stopped weeping. Had she really babbled deliriously that she loved him? Sighing, Kelly had no idea whether she had imagined it all or not. Apparently the drug that Hassad's men had used on her had had severe side effects. She was lucky to be alive.

"Mrs. Tyler?" the nurse called softly from the door.

Kelly lifted her chin. Mrs. Tyler? Perplexity showed in her eyes. "Yes?"

"Your husband's here. The doctor says you can have one visitor tonight for fifteen minutes only."

She opened her mouth and then shut it. Husband? Sam, her husband? What was going on? She moistened her healing lips, eager and yet frightened to see Sam. Her heartbeat rose with joy as he walked in and she met his intense cobalt gaze. Had it been five days since she had last seen him? Oh, God, he looked so handsome . . . so vital and alive! "Sam?" her voice quavered.

He wore the same white coveralls, although they were clean this time. There were dark shadows beneath his eyes and it appeared he had lost some weight. But an easy smile tugged at his mouth when he saw her. As he approached her bed, he held out a small bouquet of violets. "Here, these are for you."

Shyly, Kelly reached out, her fingers making contact with his hand. "Thank you," she whispered, unable to meet his burning gaze.

Sam drew up a chair and sat down. "You look better, Kelly."

"The flowers, Sam . . . they're beautiful. Where . . . how did you get them?"

A faint smile crossed his exhausted features. "They have a few florist shops here in Abu Dhabi, you know. Just because we're in a desert, that doesn't mean nothing grows." He squeezed her hand gently. "How are you feeling?"

She gave a slight shrug. "Would it sound bold if I said I was missing you?"

"No," he answered slowly. "In fact, I've missed you too, my redhaired witch." He cupped her chin, forcing her to look at him. The silence lengthened between them as he studied her thin features. "I damn near lost you, Kelly," he said huskily. "The evening we flew you in here, they said you didn't stand a chance. No one gave you any hope except Coots and I." He became more sober. "I've never prayed so hard in my life, Kelly." He allowed his hand to drop from her chin. "In fact, I never prayed much before seven days ago," he admitted.

Tears surged to her eyes. "Oh, Sam," she cried.

He got to his feet, bent over and held her for a long, long moment. Kelly's tears flowed down her cheeks and she lifted her face, longing to feel the warmth of his body against her own. "Hold me," she whispered. "Just hold me, Sam."

"Forever, if you want," he said huskily next to her ear. His voice had cracked and tears flowed down his cheeks, soaking into her beautiful copper-colored hair. He stroked her silken hair, shutting his eyes tightly, resting his head against her. For long moments he gently massaged her back and shoulders in a movement meant to relax her. For this moment she was a part of him no matter what the future might hold.

Finally, Kelly raised her head. A smile touched her wet lips as she reached up, drying his tears with the palm of her hand. "I . . . I've never seen a man cry before, Sam," she noted, her voice thick, raspy. It left her shaken, touched beyond words. A strange, fluttering sensation pulsed in her heart as she realized that Sam's tears were a sign of true strength and not a weakness. He was secure enough in his masculinity to entrust his gentle side to her. The revelation humbled Kelly as nothing else had in her life.

Sam pulled out his handkerchief and handed it to her so she could dry her flushed cheeks. "Some things in life are worth crying over, honey," he returned gently. "Like you, for instance."

She lowered her lashes, and when she raised them there was a glint of laughter in her eyes. "What's this about my being Mrs. Tyler?"

Sam's grin matched her own. "Why? Don't you like the sound of it? Kelly Tyler has a more adventurous ring to it than Kelly Blanchard."

She knotted the handkerchief between her slender fingers, unable to speak. The idea of being his wife created a warm glow in her heart. "Don't tell me I said, 'I do' when I was dying. I know! Someone gave me the last rites and you decided to marry me for my millions, right?" she teased.

He became sober. "You're close," he murmured. "The father was here and he did give you the last rites, Kelly."

Her heart plummeted. "No . . ." My God, had she truly almost died?

"I might tease you about many things, but I'd never lie to you, honey. The priest gave you the last rites while I was holding your hand. Coots was here too."

She tried to swallow the lump in her throat. "And the rest of it?" she asked softly.

"My idea. We don't know how much influence Sheik Hassad holds here in Abu Dhabi. If he thought about stealing you again, he might think twice if you had a Mrs. tacked onto your name." An irrepressible smile lurked in his azure eyes. "What if I had married you? What would you have done?"

Kelly raised her chin, meeting his gaze. "My only regret would be that we hadn't given each other a proper amount of time to get to know one another," she admitted.

Sam pursed his mouth. "Ahh, my redhaired witch has a grain of common sense after all."

"I came by it the hard way, Sam. I married Todd on the spur of the moment and lived to regret it. I spent four years in hell and I don't ever want to duplicate that mistake."

He gave a nod of his head. "Well put." He sighed. "And I agree, time does make the difference."

"Mr. Tyler?" the nurse called from the door. "I'm sorry, time's up for this evening."

Sam frowned, slowly rising. He reached out and touched her hair in a wistful motion. "Listen, I'm in town for the weekend. I'll write down the hotel and room number where I'm staying. If you feel up to it, call me later and we'll talk more of what happened."

"And then what? What about my pipe? How is it holding up?" she asked.

Sam shook his head. "I don't believe it. You've damn near just died and here you are asking how your pipe's holding up." His eyes grew misty for a moment. "You're quite a lady, you know that? And to answer your hardheaded business question, your pipe is doing just fine. We've got the water going through at high pressure now and it's working like a champ. Satisfied?"

She rested her cheek against his callused hand. "Yes," she murmured. "Come and see me tomorrow?"

Sam leaned down, his breath warm against her face. "Wild horses won't stop me," he promised huskily. He claimed her parted, waiting lips, felt her heated response. But, fearing he would hurt her, he eased the pressure and reluctantly drew away. "Be sure to have the nurse put those violets in water, honey. And every time you look at them, think of me."

Kelly was standing in the solarium of the hospital when Sam arrived the next evening. She was dressed in a light cotton gown and matching robe of pale green, a gift from Sam. Her hair, unbound and free, made her look as wild and free as the mustangs he had seen on the dry Texas panhandle. Sam halted at the entrance, admiring her as she stood near the window that overlooked the city. He could see that she was almost herself again.

"You know you're causing a riot walking up and down the halls like that?" he asked, watching her turn. A jolt of pleasure coursed through him as he saw the surprise in her emerald eyes change to unabashed happiness.

Joy surged through Kelly and she went into his waiting arms, pressing her body fully against him. "Sam," she whispered breathlessly. She didn't care what he thought. It had been a long, boring day and she had missed him terribly. If he was surprised by her spontaneity, he took it in stride. His arms wrapped around her slender form, crushing her against him.

"I've missed you," he growled. "Come here," he ordered. He kissed her slowly and as he traced the outline of her lips, he felt her melt against him. He invaded the sweet depths of her mouth. A soft moan rose in her throat and he reveled in her uninhibited passion. Kelly broke away first, her laughter the tinkle of bells as she looked up at him. Her eyes . . . He groaned to himself. Her eyes were shining with life as never before. And he knew he was partly responsible for it.

"I never thought you'd get here!" she confided, taking his hand and pulling him from the solarium to the adjacent tiled balcony.

"Oh?" he asked, allowing himself to be tugged along. "Where are you taking me?"

Kelly laughed. The fresh salt air from the Persian Gulf lifted strands of hair from her shoulders as she rested her elbows on the balustrade. "Look, Sam! Isn't it beautiful? The salt air. The minarets! I never realized how beautiful this city was." She turned to him, gazing up into his handsome, craggy features. In the last twenty-four hours a miracle had occurred. No longer did Sam look exhausted. The tautness of his skin was gone. There was color in his face, his blue eyes were lively with humor once again.

"You're certainly feeling your oats tonight," he noted with a careless grin. "What's the occasion?"

"The doctors are releasing me. They've given me a clean bill of health." She giggled like a schoolgirl. "I think I'm driving them all crazy! I pace my room. I pace the halls. I can't speak Arabic."

Sam reached over, drawing her into the crook of his arm. "You're getting restless."

Kelly nodded. "I've made a decision, Sam."

"You have?"

"Yes. I'm going to fly back on that helicopter with you tomorrow morning."

His brows drew together and he put her at arm's length. "What are you talking about?" he growled.

Kelly braced herself. "I'm going back to the blowout, Sam. No one's recorded any data on that pipe. I need at least one week to put together some sort of test results to see—"

"Dammit!" he exploded, gripping her shoulders. "I won't allow it!"

Kelly stood stunned, openmouthed. His fingers were like brands on her arms.

"Now you look here," he ground out softly. "Hassad is still in the area. We've got reported terrorist activity which is keeping him busy chasing them, but he'll be back. It's hotter than hell out there right now, Kelly. You suffered a sunstroke. A sunstroke can kill you. We don't have facilities at the site to take care of you if you have a relapse."

She drew herself up and stepped away from him. "I'll be okay, Sam." Her voice took on a new note of stubbornness. "You forget, my life doesn't begin and end in this desert. I have a multimillion-dollar business to salvage when I get back home, providing Blanchard pipe withstands the tests this time." Her eyes pleaded with him. "Sam . . . don't you see? Whether I want to or not, I've got to go back out there! I'm scared. Yes, I'm scared as hell. Every time I think of Hassad I . . . I . . ."

Sam swore, his eyes black with anger. "You damn near got raped! Not to mention getting kidnapped! And you want to go back on site and invite his advances again? Where is your brain, Kelly?"

"I'll wear a pistol on me at all times! If I see Hassad, I'll shoot him myself!" she flung back. "I'm going and that's all there is to it!"

His nostrils flared in silent fury as he glared at her. "Okay," he finally muttered, "have it your way. I'll be back in ten minutes." He turned on his heel and stalked off the terrace.

Kelly trembled, suddenly cold even though the evening was warm. She saw the mixture of hurt, anger and anguish in his eyes. She heard it in his voice. Shutting her eyes tightly, Kelly turned, hugging the balustrade for security. She loved him. God, how much she loved that man! But her father's reputation was at stake. She had to tough it out no matter how frightened she really felt down inside. She acknowledged her fear of Hassad. But she wouldn't allow fear to stop her.

She was walking slowly back to her room when she saw Sam stalking toward her. His face was set and taciturn as he approached her.

"Come on," he ordered tightly. "You're coming with me." His fingers closed about her arm and he forced her along with him.

Despite her protests, Sam hauled Kelly back into her room. Her only suitcase had been thrown unceremoniously on top of the bed and opened. Sam slammed the door, breathing hard. "Now you get dressed and pack whatever articles you want to bring with you," he ordered.

She glared at him, hands resting imperiously on her hips. "Just who the hell do you think you are?" she shouted. "I'm not taking orders from you!"

"You don't have any option," he breathed angrily.

"Now you either get dressed or I'll haul you out of here just like you are."

Kelly blinked. He was serious. "Where are we going?"

"To my hotel room."

She opened her mouth and then shut it. "Your room?"

"That's right. You'll stay in my sight until tomorrow morning."

Kelly tensed. "And then?"

"Then I'm putting you on a plane going Stateside."

Her green eyes narrowed. He was serious. Controlling her initial burst of anger, she considered her options. One look at his set features convinced her he meant to carry through with his plan whether she cooperated or not. "Give me ten minutes, will you? I don't want you standing there staring at me while I dress!"

A crooked smile fled across his mouth. "Okay, ten minutes. But if you're not ready—"

"I'll be ready! Just get out of here, Sam Tyler!"

There was a continued tension between them as they took a taxi to the Hilton Hotel. Kelly sat stiffly in one corner of the cab. Sam sat infuriatingly silent in the other corner. He took a grip on her arm once they arrived at the hotel, and in the elevator, he slid his arm around her waist even though there were five other passengers with them. He wouldn't put it past Kelly to try to slip out on another floor and leave him empty-handed.

Once in his room, he locked the door and put the key in his pocket. She stood there, devastatingly beautiful and absolutely furious. He placed her suitcase on a small bureau.

"You might as well get comfortable," he growled. "You aren't going anywhere until eight A.M. tomorrow morning."

Kelly's eyes rounded with disbelief. "Like to tell me where I'm going at eight A.M.?"

Sam congratulated himself with a slight smile. He walked over to the small refrigerator and drew out a bottle of chilled champagne. "You're booked on a flight for Houston. I intend to make sure you're on board."

"You bastard!" she breathed. "I won't allow anyone to run my life for me."

He gave her a cool glance and popped the cork on the bottle. "Under ordinary circumstances, I'd agree with you." He poured the frothy liquid into two glasses. "Has it ever entered your mind that I care about keeping your skin in one piece even if you don't?"

"It's my skin and you don't own me!"

"I'd never want to own you, Kelly. But I would hope that you trust my intentions where you're concerned enough to listen to my judgment."

She gave him a frosty stare. He was so damn sure of himself. And of her. In the back of her mind she knew that he was only doing what he thought best. But right now, that was secondary.

"My decision-making process is not faulty, Sam! I told you, I'm scared to go back there but—"

"Duty calls?" he finished, handing her the glass.

Kelly placed the champagne on the coffee table. "I owe you my life," she breathed, "but I meant it when I said you can't run it for me, Sam."

He met her fiery gaze. "I'm collecting on that debt today," he said. "I'm asking for one day of your time in exchange for your life." His voice hardened. "That's my demand. And that's the way it'll be, Kelly."

Sam caught her arm as she tried to slap him. Calmly he put his glass down, then returned all his attention to her. He couldn't be angry at her outburst. He would have felt the same. He captured her in his arms. "Calm down," he growled. "You've got nothing to be angry over. I'm doing you a favor."

Kelly muttered a string of expletives that raised even his eyebrows. "You damn roughneck! Let me go! I'll show you! No one runs my life for me! You hear me, Sam Tyler! Oh," she cried, realizing it was useless to struggle, "damn you . . . damn . . ."

Sam ran his fingers through her reddish gold hair. "You're such a Texas wildcat," he murmured. "A real hellion of the first order."

Kelly struggled briefly once more, wildly aware of his body. She refused to meet his searching blue eyes. "Let me go," she demanded breathlessly.

Sam changed position, smiling silently. "And let you nail me with a right hook?"

"I won't try to hit you again," she gritted out.

He enjoyed the rise and fall of her breasts beneath the simple white blouse she wore. Her nostrils were flared with indignation, her hair in disarray and still her stubborness continued unabated. "I think it's about time someone tried to gentle you," he murmured, catching her startled look. He stroked her flushed cheek with the back of his hand. "Tamed," he whispered huskily, "not broken. Now come here and quit fighting me."

Kelly swallowed her protests as his mouth moved lightly across her lips in a breath-stealing kiss. It was a kiss meant to inflame, arouse and coax. His mouth moved with skilled assurance, teasing, outlining her lips. A moan broke from her throat even as she tried to free herself. His mouth hardened, taking charge of her, forcing her to give in to the fire that licked through her body. She was starving for his touch, and the feel of his well-muscled body against her own made her ache with need. Suddenly, all the danger Kelly had faced in the past week melted away beneath his skillful hands. Hadn't this been what she had wanted all along? To love and be loved by Sam Tyler?

The ache of desire intensified as his hand lightly caressed her taut, straining breast. The nipple hardened beneath his coaxing. "Love me, Sam. Please, love me. I need you so . . ."

A curious flame flickered in his eyes as he stared down at her. "I've been dreaming of loving you since the day I met you," he breathed hoarsely. "I almost lost you, Kelly. I won't lose you again," he whispered against her lips.

She closed her eyes as he lifted her off her feet and into his arms. He gently placed her on the bed and proceeded to undress her. His hands, so large, scarred and callused, gently caressed her as if she were a fragile, priceless treasure. She felt his fingers tremble as he removed her blouse. As the lacy bra slipped away, he grazed her breasts with his palm. A soft sigh of pleasure escaped from her. She leaned upward, placing small, fiery kisses from his jaw, down his corded neck to the wiry hair on his broad chest. His groan vibrated through her being. Sam made her feel more womanly than she ever had before.

He nudged the slacks off her hips and she shivered with delight as his hands roved down the length of her legs. Each touch added fuel to the fire, building her need of him into a near frenzy. He leaned over, placing feathery kisses across her stomach while removing the panties. His long fingers traced her beautifully formed thighs, parting them, caressing the heated place between.

She moaned his name, her breasts rising and falling with shallow gasps as he eased his bulk across her body. Placing his knee between her thighs, he sought out her gaze.

"You're mine," he whispered fiercely, sealing her lips with a branding kiss meant to make her his forever. She arched against him, begging him to complete the union.

"Now," she whispered, her voice tremulous, "please love me now, Sam. Take me, I need you so badly. Please . . ."

He slid his large hand beneath the curve of her hip, bringing her upward. His body trembled with barely controlled desire. He checked himself, not wanting to hurt her. She moaned and gently he invaded the sweet, moist depths of her being. He felt her tense and halted momentarily. Tears wet her thick auburn lashes, spilling down the sides of her face. Her eyes . . . oh, God, her eyes were shining with love. He felt himself close to exploding; he wanted to bury himself in her. But no, not this first time. Life was too precious, too short for them. He wanted her to feel pleasure, not pain over their first union. She had felt enough pain because of her first marriage.

"It's all right, Sam," she whispered. It had been so long . . . so long. How could she tell him that Todd had made her shudder when he touched her? She had welcomed the divorce, had wanted no man to touch her again. Not until now. It had been over a year since her body had slid into dormancy. But Sam was coaxing her senses into new life.

A tender smile curved his mouth. "It will be, honey," he promised, slowly bringing her into rhythm with him.

"Just relax, let me help . . . it'll be good for both of us. . . ."

She closed her eyes, seeking, finding his strong, cherishing mouth. The momentary discomfort soon gave way to pleasure and she arched fully against his strong, virile body. Somewhere in the spiraling world of happiness they found together, she climaxed violently, and a wild cry tore from her lips. She fell back, completely sated, fulfilled and loved. Moments later, she felt him tense, too. A low growl came from him as he clutched her tightly to him. A tender smile touched her lips when he brought her against him afterward. Her fiery red curls spilled out across the dark mat of hair on his chest.

She tasted the salt on his jaw as she placed small kisses on the corners of his mouth. Her heart had blossomed fully and all she wanted to do was share the aftermath of the joy he had brought to her. Barely opening his eyes, Sam pulled her damp form on top of him. A smile lingered on his face as he looked up at her.

"Has anyone ever told you how loving you are, Kelly Blanchard?" he asked huskily, tracing the curve of her damp cheek.

Kelly barely shook her head. "No," she whispered.

Sam ran his hand down her long, beautifully formed back. His hand came to rest on her nicely rounded rear. "You give everything you have, honey. You don't hold back. That's rare. But then," he murmured "you are one in a million." And how he loved her for that! But the admission remained frozen on the tip of his tongue. It was too soon to tell her. She needed time to think about him, about them.

Kelly smiled indulgently, tracing the outline of his

mouth with her fingertip. "You're a gentle giant, Sam Tyler," she said huskily. "And you know something?"

"No, what?"

"You are indeed a tamer of women."

"Just redheaded witches," he corrected. "Come here, let me hold you for a while."

She complied with his request, allowing him to position her next to his body, with his arms around her keeping her safe. Always safe. . . .

9

Coots Matthews wiped his sweaty brow with the back of his hand and squinted through the heat waves. The blowout continued to roar behind him as he turned toward the approaching figure. Sam Tyler's face was stony, his blue eyes narrowed slits of barely contained anger.

"Where is she?" Tyler yelled above the noise.

"Kelly?"

"Who the hell else did you think I meant?"

Coots grinned slightly. "You might as well settle down, Sam. She's been hard at work ever since the chopper dropped her off six hours ago." He looked Tyler up and down. "You don't look any the worse for wear. What happened? She give you the slip?"

Sam muttered a curse. "Yes. Is Kelly at the pipe monitoring equipment?"

Coots nodded. "Yeah. Let her stay there. I got Colly watch'n over her. I need you here. We're about ready to make a dry run with the blowout preventer attached on the hook of the athey wagon. I want you to direct the operation."

"What about that sheik?"

"The government's still got him chasing guerillas." Coots patted him on the shoulder. "Don't worry, he'll leave us alone."

Sam's mouth thinned. "The bastard had better stay away."

Coots nodded. "Don't worry, he will."

Sam glared in the direction of the three large pools of water. He could make out the figures of Kelly and Colly in the distance. Just wait until I get my hands on you, Kelly, he promised to himself. Disgruntled, Sam walked toward the trailers, which were now surrounded by a cyclone-type fence with concertina barbed wire at the top. More than anything else, he was angry at himself for allowing Kelly to slip out of the hotel room as he slept. After seven restless nights and the exertion of making love with her, he had fallen into an exhausted sleep. The last thing Sam remembered was Kelly's warm, yielding body next to his.

Growling an epithet, he climbed the steps of the shack and went inside. Coots drank deeply from a jug of water and then passed it over to him.

"We got phase two completed, Sam. We're finished digging that twelve-foot hole around the pipe. Colly and Boots used steel cable attached to two bulldozers to saw off the gas pipe. We got a smooth surface to work with now. I just got the blowout preventer wrapped in asbestos and foil to protect it from the heat." He gave Sam a slap on the shoulder. "Kelly looks pretty good considering everything."

"Well, she's going to get her rear paddled before the day's over. Damn her bullheadedness."

Coots chuckled drily, a broad Texan grin spreading across his face. "She's got spunk. A real hellcat."

Sam became serious. "You sure Hassad won't be around?"

"He'll stay away. 'Sides, Boots told the government officials that if they didn't keep Hassad away from our site, we'd pack up and leave. I think that convinced them we meant business."

"Good," he growled, reaching for his dusty construction hat. Throwing it on his head, he said, "Let's get that preventer stationed. There's a certain redhaired witch I want to have a confrontation with later."

Kelly had just completed her initial research. Earlier she had watched the helicopter land and had prepared herself to meet his angry attack. But to her relief, Coots detoured him, postponing the inevitable showdown.

Colly was paged on the hand-held radio he carried. He waved to Kelly.

"I'm needed at the blowout. Sam and Boots are going to try to position the preventer on that pipe."

She nodded, feeling weak beneath the harsh rays of the sun. Since she'd returned to the site, Kelly had noted subtle differences in the camp. The most important was the fact that the shacks were now guarded by government troops. That knowledge eased some of her immediate fear. Everything concerning the capping of the blowout was proceeding smoothly and she took a deep steadying breath.

"I'm going over to the shack, Colly. I'm getting tired."

He nodded. "Go ahead. We'll meet you there for supper later."

Kelly watched from the trailer window as a fifty-two-ton blowout preventer was lifted by a crane and attached to the athey wagon. A counterweight balanced the entire contraption, permitting the athey wagon to be moved forward and backward by the men on the bulldozer. Fascinated as to how they would maneuver the monstrous blowout preventer directly into the flame, Kelly watched their progress. Sam stood behind the shield next to the driver of the bulldozer. Continuous streams of water cascaded down upon them. She inhaled deeply. Thank God Blanchard pipe was standing up to the job.

Later, the extended boom angle was carefully measured and stakes were driven into the ground where the bulldozer would halt to place the blowout preventer into the flame. After the figures were dutifully recorded in Boots's notebook, everyone backed away from the roaring inferno. Kelly was exhausted but she rummaged around to locate enough canned food to make a hearty stew for the men. Her stomach was knotted in anticipation of meeting Sam. Pressing her lips together, Kelly tried to ignore the guilt she felt about sneaking out of the hotel room after Sam had fallen asleep.

The door was jerked open and Kelly gasped, spinning around. Sam stood in the doorway, glaring at her. His face was glistening with sweat; his dark hair was plastered against his forehead. He took off his hardhat and moved inside.

"You look like hell," he growled, coming around the table and closing the distance between them.

Kelly maintained her position, refusing to yield. "Well, I can't say much more for you!"

His white uniform clung to his body. "If you didn't look so damn pale, I'd take you over my knee, Kelly."

"Don't you dare try, Sam Tyler! And quit being so angry at me! You forced me to do this! I didn't want to leave you. But you got it into your head to put me on a plane against my wishes." Her green eyes narrowed.

He halted, drinking in her fiery beauty. Suddenly, all of his anger dissipated. A slight grin pulled at the corner of his mouth. "You wanted to stay longer, eh?"

She avoided his amused, provocative gaze. "Go to hell. You're just an arrogant male after all!"

He laughed, gripping her arms and bringing her against his body. "And you're an arrogant little wildcat." His smile disappeared as he studied her in the intervening silence. "You look pale. You feeling all right?"

Kelly shrugged. "Just a little tired," she lied. Actually, she had done too much the first day. She craved the sanctuary of sleep once again. But she didn't want anyone to know just how bad she felt for fear of being sent back to Abu Dhabi.

His fingers became more gentle on her arms. "Have you eaten yet?"

"No . . . I don't have much of an appetite yet, I guess."

"Come and sit down. You should take some salt tablets, eat a few bites and then hit the sack."

The encouragement in his voice gave her momentary strength. She sat across the table from him, toying idly with the stew she had made. He glanced up once. "You aren't eating."

A frown creased her brow. "Quit picking on me!"

"Now you're turning into a shrew. Why don't you go to bed?"

Kelly rose. "I will. Goodnight, Sam. And"—she chewed on her lower lip—"I'm sorry I left you. I didn't want to but . . ."

He nodded. "I know why you did, Kelly. I don't agree with it, but that doesn't matter right now." He wanted to add, I'm just concerned about losing you. "Lock your door this time."

She grimaced. "Don't worry, I will!"

She slept restlessly, kicking off the light cover over her. The noise of the blowout roared across the landscape, the light from the gigantic red and yellow torch making it seem like daylight outside the complex. Once she woke with a start, thinking that she heard Hassad's men sneaking into her room. The dancing shadows on the walls were a reflection of the blowout. Emotionally exhausted and physically weak, Kelly put her head down once more on the uncomfortable pillow, willing herself to sleep.

What seemed like moments later, Kelly sat upright, awakened by her own screams. Horrified, disoriented, she sobbed.

"Kelly!"

Wildly, she looked around the room.

"Kelly! Open up!"

Sam. It was Sam's voice! Choking on a sob, she got to her feet and flew to the door. Hands shaking badly, Kelly finally managed to unlock it. The door was jerked open and she stood forlornly in front of Sam. His face was tense, his eyes filled with worry as he anxiously looked at her. Dressed in only a pair of briefs, he held a .357 magnum revolver in his hand, ready to use it.

Tears coursed down her cheeks and she uttered a little cry and fell into his open arms. "Oh, Sam," she sobbed, burying her head against his chest. "It was horrible! Horrible!" she cried.

She was aware of other men's voices in the background and Sam replying. He led her over to her sleeping mat after closing the door behind him.

"Come on," he soothed, "lie down here with me. You're just having bad dreams, honey. Sshh, it's all right. I'm here and no one is going to hurt you."

She sought the protection of his body and her weeping gradually abated. Sam gently removed the damp, tangled strands of auburn hair from her wet cheeks. He lay with his back against the wall, her head resting on his shoulder. She shuddered convulsively.

"You're safe," Sam whispered against her ear. "Come on, relax, Kelly. Hassad isn't here. We probably woke you up when we came in the shack a while ago. I'm sorry."

She swallowed against a lump in her throat. Gradually, she remembered hearing the low murmur of men's voices. In her nightmare-ridden state she had confused Sam and the others for Hassad's men. "I'm sorry, Sam," she said brokenly. "God, I feel like such a baby . . . I'm just not like this. . . ."

"It isn't every day you get drugged and kidnapped, either," he responded drily. "You're being a little too hard on yourself under the circumstances." He leaned over and pressed a light kiss on her temple. "When I came back from Nam I had nightmares that lasted for years."

She sniffed. "Really?"

"Really." He ran his hand over her sweaty body, noting that her nightgown was completely soaked. "Let me get you a dry gown or you'll catch pneumonia."

"Don't leave me!" she begged. "Not yet . . ."

Sam relaxed, pulling the dry coverlet up across her shoulders and tucking it around her back, hips and long legs. "I'll stay as long as you want, honey," he soothed, embracing her gently. "Just close your eyes and sleep."

The beat of his heart calmed her. The figure of Hassad receded from her weary mind and Kelly nuzzled against Sam. Safe at last, she fell into a heavy slumber.

Kelly awoke to the same steady heartbeat that had helped her to sleep. During the night, she had pressed herself against Sam and had thrown one leg carelessly across his own. Her arm spanned the breadth of his torso; her head was tucked beneath his chin, her reddish gold hair streaming across his chest. She still felt exhausted from the terrors of the night. Sam's hand rested protectively on her shoulder and his breathing was soft and shallow. He was still asleep. Languorously, Kelly opened her green eyes, her gaze following the solid line of his chin. Sam's face was relaxed and almost boyish looking in sleep. A tender smile curved her mouth as she silently thanked him for holding her all night.

The roar of the blowout continued unabated in the background. The rays of the sun were slanting into the room at a low angle, indicating that it was probably around six A.M. Sam stirred, his hand brushing the curve of her breast, then coming to rest upon her ribcage. Slowly, he opened his blue eyes. Strands of dark hair lay across his forehead. Kelly reached up, running her slender fingers through the strands, and brushed them back into place.

"Good morning," she whispered, her lips a mere inch from his mouth.

He gazed at her through half opened lids. "It is," he agreed, his voice still thick with sleep. "This is the way it should have been," he muttered.

"What?" she asked, a smile lingering in her eyes.

"Yesterday morning when I woke up. You weren't there. I expected to wake up and see you sleeping in my arms."

She leaned forward, her lips brushing his strong, masculine mouth. A shiver coursed through her as she felt him slide his hand upward to caress her breast. "I had other plans, Sam Tyler," she told him throatily.

He smiled, rising up on one arm and tucking her into the curve of his body. Her red hair flowed across the pillow, making her skin appear paler than ever. "I've got a few plans myself," he admitted, tracing the curve of her cheek with his finger. "And you're included in them." He caressed her shapely lips "Whether you like it or not."

"Don't start giving me ultimatums!" She was up in one fluid motion. "You ought to know by now, that doesn't work."

A lazy grin pulled at his mouth. "I love it when you get angry. Do you realize your eyes are like an incredible green fire?" Sam reached up and pulled her back into his arms. He pressed his mouth insistently to her lips and felt her response. Her lips were soft, searching, parting beneath his mouth like the petals of a flower. Gradually, he raised his head so that he could study the gold flecks in her wide, lustrous eyes. "That's better," he growled. He wanted to make love with her again, but this wasn't the time or the place.

"I've got to go in a minute," he said. "Kelly, there's something that's been bothering me and I want to ask you about it."

She nodded. Her body craved more of his kisses. The memory of their lovemaking a day before swept through her like white-hot lava. No man had ever made her feel more alive, more of a woman, and she knew that her love for Sam had much to do with it. "What?" she asked, her voice wispy.

He rested his hand near her hip. "That first day I met you, I saw Gage Wallace drive up as I was leaving. And then the second time I came to your office, he was with you again." His hand tightened on her waist. "Does he mean something to you, Kelly?"

Her features contorted and she struggled to sit up. "Oh, he means something all right. Sam, he maneuvered my ex-husband out of their partnership in our steel company. And then he tried to court me, which made Todd jealous."

Sam ran his hand down her bare arm. "Care to tell me about it?"

Her lips set in a grim line. "Wallace would deliberately come over to my father's regional office, which I managed, to make Todd envious. He tried to get Todd to think we were having an affair!" Her voice shook with disgust.

"Were you?"

"I'm not sure that even deserves an answer!"

"You get angry in a hurry, woman."

She allowed herself to be mollified by his teasing tone. "The answer is no. He's a slick businessman, Sam. His morals are worse than a snake's. Sure, his steel company is one of the few in the United States making big profits. But I'd hate to tell you how he gets those profits!"

"Other than the tie with your ex-husband, what does Wallace have to do with you now?"

Kelly pushed the hair away from her face in a gesture of annoyance. "The second time he visited, when you came in to tell me about the blowout, Gage had the audacity to suggest I marry him." She looked up at the ceiling in furious silence.

"Why did he suggest that?"

"He said Blanchard Pipe's image had suffered in the marketplace. Our credibility was damaged beyond repair because of the pipe failures we had. He sweetly suggested that he buy into my father's company to salvage it and then marry me too. Convenient, isn't it?"

Sam's brows furrowed. "Yes," he murmured, trying to make sense of Wallace's activities. He caught Kelly's indignant look. "Well, are you going to sell him shares or marry him?" he goaded, a hint of mirth in his voice.

Kelly glared at him. "Sometimes, Sam Tyler, I think you get immense pleasure out of teasing me unmercifully," she declared between clenched teeth.

His grin widened. "You're so easy to tease. You're like fifty pounds of dynamite ready to go off on a second's notice."

Smiling, Kelly reached over and placed her slender

hand on his shoulder. Each time she touched him, a pang of longing went through her. "The answer is no to both your questions."

"I expected as much."

"Oh, stop being so arrogant!"

"You wouldn't have it any other way, Kelly Blanchard. Now quit spitting and clawing for two seconds and come here."

This time, he kissed her deeply, stoking the fires within her. Satisfied, Sam raised his head. There was a tender light in his eyes as he watched her. "Listen," he began huskily. "Today you stay in the shack and rest. You're not well yet. I'll have someone go over to the gauges and read them for you. No more sun for you, woman. Not until I say so. Understand?"

Kelly's breathing was shallow, her heart was beating wildly in her breast, and her body ached to fulfill the needs that Sam had effortlessly coaxed to life within her. "Yes," she whispered, "I'll stay here today."

Giving an approving nod of his head, Sam stood and then placed the thin blanket across her. "Good. I'll be back over here in a few hours to check on you."

She slept again after Sam had left. The next time she awoke, it was almost noon. After changing into her white coveralls, Kelly padded out into the main area of the porta-camp. She looked out the window and saw that they were beginning to position the heavily wrapped blowout preventer over the roaring flame. Forgetting that she was both hungry and thirsty, Kelly stood mesmerized by the spectacle.

Sam directed the bulldozer that was pushing the

unmanned athey wagon forward. At the stake, they halted the bulldozer. Five water monitors continuously spewed thousands of gallons of water upon the flame. Kelly tensed as the crane hook carrying the preventer was nudged into the roaring fire. Flames exploded in all directions as the massive apparatus hung over the blowout. The men's actions were smooth and carefully calculated as Sam positioned the crane at just the right angle.

Kelly had no idea how Sam could know exactly where to place the preventer. But when Sam gave the final hand signal, Kelly watched in amazement as the blowout preventer slid over the pipe. The raging fire now shot out the top of it. Taking a deep, shaky breath, Kelly realized the worst was over. All that remained to be done now was welding the preventer to the pipe. After that, they would begin to control the blowout by capping the main fire and redirecting it into the smaller pipes located on each side of the preventer. At no time would they allow the flame to be extinguished. If they did, the H2S gas would kill everyone working at the wellhead.

It was almost three in the afternoon before Sam managed to get away from the welding job on the pipe. Kelly's heart pounded when he entered the trailer. Taking off his hardhat, Sam cast a look in her direction.

"How are you feeling?" he asked.

Kelly had never realized just how brutally demanding the job of an oil well firefighter was until now. Sam's face was glistening with sweat, his dark hair plastered to his skull, the coveralls clinging to his muscled body. "Better. You were right. I needed to rest today."

He opened the small refrigerator, digging out several pieces of fresh meat and the leftover stew from the day before. "Can I get that in writing? Kelly Blanchard admitting that maybe someone besides herself has a good idea?"

Kelly laughed with him. "Here, I'll fry the meat." She looked at it more closely. "What kind of meat is that?"

Sam handed it to her. "Goat."

She wrinkled her nose. "Oh."

He left her to the kitchen duties and sat down at the table, where he drank nearly a quart of water. "Damn, what I'd do for a cold beer."

"I noticed the absence of liquor around here," Kelly observed.

"Yeah, it's against the Moslem laws to consume liquor. If you get caught, it's a jail sentence. And if you can get it on the black market, it costs around eighty American dollars for a quart of whiskey." He shrugged. "I'll just be damned happy to wrap this particular well up and get back to Texas," he said good-naturedly. He sat back, watching her work over the old, dilapidated gas stove. Kelly had piled her thick mane of hair high on her head with feminine-looking pink combs. Tendrils had escaped to fall around her face, giving her an ethereal look. Sam watched her worriedly. Her peach-colored skin was almost transparent and he couldn't ignore the shadows beneath her emerald eyes.

"Boots and Coots don't anticipate any trouble with the pipe, Kelly. Colly's bringing up the gauge readings in a while." He toyed with the salt shaker on the table, choosing his words carefully. "You know, in another three days at the most, we'll be finished here."

Kelly fried the goat steaks as if they were beef steak.

The odor was different, but not unappetizing. "That's good," she commented, smiling. "I'm dreaming of a hot bath."

"You could have it earlier, you know. . . ."

She gave a stubborn shake of her head. "I'm going to stick it out, Sam."

His mouth became a grim line and he withheld a few well-chosen expletives. In no time Kelly had finished cooking the goat meat and made him a fresh pot of coffee.

Kelly sat opposite him, happy despite the stark surroundings. Had she ever enjoyed Todd's company like this? No, a voice answered. There was something pleasurable in watching Sam wolf down the food. He enjoys life, she thought. Just like he enjoys me. She frowned, suddenly feeling alarm. The love she felt for Sam was all-consuming. She craved his company, treasured the time simply spent conversing with him. But did he need her as a bed partner only? Was that all he wanted from her? Or did he want something more? She wished with all her heart that she could remember those fragmented days of delirium in the hospital at Abu Dhabi. Had he said he loved her? Or was it simply her drugged brain making it all up?

She stole a look up at him only to discover he was watching her. A blush stained her cheeks.

"Do you always stare?" she challenged.

"When something's worth staring at, yes."

"Well . . ." she muttered, "it's embarrassing."

A smile tugged at the corners of his mouth. "Your ex-husband was a fool," Sam decided. "No man in his right mind would ever leave you."

Nervously, Kelly entwined her fingers. "Most men don't feel the way you do, Sam. Thank you for the compliment anyway. It does my sagging ego good."

Sam rose to his feet. "Like I said, I'll be glad when we get back to Houston," he repeated enigmatically.

Kelly gazed up at him, her lips slightly parted. "Sam . . . I need to know something."

He halted. "Sure. Anything."

Kelly swallowed hard. "That confrontation with Gage last time. From the look on your face you knew him. . . ."

Sam grimaced. "Unfortunately, yes, Kelly. After Fay divorced me, she met Wallace. He strung her along and she ended up getting hurt by him. Fay comes from a very rich oil family and Wallace courted her with an ulterior motive." His eyes narrowed in memory of those times. "She was vulnerable and hurting. Wallace walked right in and after five dates with her, professed he loved her." He spat out the words. "The bastard would have married her to get to her money. It was as simple as that."

Kelly chewed on her lower lip. Sam didn't believe in overnight love . . . and that was all that they shared. A new sense of despair washed over her and she tried to hide the hurt beginning to ache within her. "What did you do?" she asked faintly.

"I was finally able to talk some sense into Fay. Wallace had gone so far as to buy an engagement ring for her. I gave him some ultimatums that he didn't appreciate. Since then, we're like two pit bulls around one another. He knows I'd take great pleasure in beating the hell out of him."

* * *

Kelly remained in the trailer throughout the next three days, going out into the desert to read the gauges on the water monitors only when necessary. Soon, the blowout preventer was welded to the pipe and the fire was rerouted through the arms. Smaller flames roared out across the desert away from the main area. Kelly watched with mixed feelings as the H2S gas was harnessed and capped. The desert suddenly grew silent. The men of Boots and Coots tiredly looked at one another. Coots Matthews gave new orders and soon the reloading of their equipment was begun. By the evening of the next day, they would all be back in Houston. Kelly's green eyes were shadowed with regret and anguish.

Had her brief affair with Sam been only that? He had made no attempt to sleep with her again since the first evening when she had had nightmares. Of course, that was understandable in the present circumstances, she told herself. There was no privacy in the shack. But he rarely touched her now and never kissed her. A growing coldness in the pit of her stomach made her feel nauseous. She would get back to Houston and take up the management of her father's company. Blanchard Pipe had stood the test. All that remained was for her office manager to bring her the lab's test results to find out why that one order of pipe had failed out in the field. Kelly turned away from the window, feeling depressed. She should feel excited about going home, but she didn't. Her heart was aching with a loss she knew would come very shortly. Closing her eyes, Kelly pressed her hand against her chest. What a fool she had been, falling so artlessly in love with Sam Tyler! At her age, blind love was the result of sheer stupidity, not ignorance. And yet, she could feel no regret for her actions, because Sam had shown her that she was worthy of a man's attention. He had shown her she was a woman with a capacity for feeling that even she had not suspected.

10

ou aren't going to like what I have to show you,
Kelly," Jake warned. He watched her walk across the
office, remaining silent until she seated herself. She
appeared wan and drawn. It left him feeling guilty about
discussing the information from the lab analysis.

Kelly forced a slight smile. She should have taken
another day off after her return to Houston. But she
couldn't bear to remain at home with the pain of her
memories.

During those last twenty-four hours with Sam, time
had been at a premium. In the C-130 cargo plane she
had slept in his arms. Each touch of his hands on her
body was indelibly branded into her memory. When they
finally reached Houston International, Sam had pulled
her aside before the flurry of activity commenced.

"Go on home, Kelly," he ordered, his eyes broadcast-
ing his concern.

She stared up into his strong face which was lined with exhaustion. "What about you?" she demanded.

He gave her a slight smile. "We'll have at least four hours of unloading to do here before any of us can crash. Kelly, I want to—"

"Hey, Sam!" Boots yelled.

Sam lifted his head. "What now?" he growled, releasing her. "Stay here, I'll be right back," he told her.

She had stood, arms wrapped around herself, suddenly chilled even though the temperature was in the high eighties. In comparison to the Rub al Khali Desert, eighty was cool! She watched as Sam talked with Boots and Coots for several minutes, then broke free and walked toward her.

His face was set, an unhappy expression in his eyes. He gripped her arm when he reached her. "Bad news," he said. "We've just got a call to go down to Venezuela. They got an offshore platform that's on fire and they want us to put it out. Damn." He studied her intently. "Will you be all right, Kelly?"

The worry in his voice made her heart turn over. "Of course. You know we redheaded witches survive very well on our own." It was a total lie. All she wanted to do was fall into his arms and sleep. She wanted to speak of her love for him. But hadn't Sam made it very clear that he didn't believe in instant attraction? She swallowed the torrent of admissions that wanted to pour from her lips.

"Sam . . ." she said breathlessly, "be careful. . . ."

His blue eyes took on a familiar teasing glint. "As long as you don't put a curse on me for running off and leaving you, I will be."

She forced a laugh for his benefit. He had no idea of the inner turmoil she was experiencing. It was just as well.

"Platforms are dangerous, Sam. Please, for God's sake, be careful." Her voice was strained with unshed tears. He pulled her into his arms, pressing her tightly against him.

"You'd miss me?"

"Oh! You arrogant—"

He laughed. "I know." He kissed her temple, resting his head on her fiery red hair. "I shouldn't tease you. You're tired and it's been one hell of an experience for you." He put her at arm's length, hungrily assessing her features. His voice lowered, sending a shiver of desire coursing through her. "We've got things to discuss when I come back, Kelly. This is not the time or place." His fingers caressed her shoulders and arms. "I don't know how long this Venezuela job will last. Just keep the home fires burning for me?"

She stifled a laugh. "Is that a pun, Sam Tyler? Or do you want me to become an arsonist to halt your world-wide globetrotting and lure you back to Houston?"

He leaned down, pressing a long, gentle kiss to her lips. She melted against his hard, muscular frame, so much clay to be molded by his will. She returned his ardent, searching kiss, wanting in some silent way to convey her love for him.

Kelly made a concerted effort to pull herself back to the present. Jake was giving her a worried look and she sat up, elbows on the desk.

"Okay, what have you found out about that batch of pipe, Jake?"

His brows drew together as he handed her the sheaf of papers. "You sure you're up to it, today? You look mighty peaked."

"I'll be okay," she lied. Her gaze immediately went to the metallurgy report. Her father had developed a precise formula for Blanchard Pipe and Kelly had memorized it long ago. According to the lab report, the amounts of the various alloys used had not been correct in that particular batch of steel. Kelly shot a look over at Jake.

"This isn't right."

"No, it isn't," Jake returned heavily. "I've alerted all the companies we've sold that pipe to and we're in the process of recalling it. I'm replacing it with a different batch. So far our investigation shows only one pipe that didn't meet our specifications. Obviously the problem was caused by the metallurgical department at the steel mill."

Kelly's mouth thinned as she perused the rest of the complicated reports. "What I don't understand is how that metallurgist could make this kind of obvious mistake! He's supposed to test the mixture a number of times before it comes out of the furnace. Damn," she breathed, throwing the papers down in front of her. Her green eyes narrowed upon Jake.

"There's more," she said, suddenly knowing he had not told her something.

"Yes, there is." He handed her another sheet of paper. "I had a detective do some investigation on the metallurgist. He turned up some pretty damning evidence. When I confronted the metallurgist about it he broke down. Apparently, someone bribed him to alter the formula."

Kelly's lips parted. She stared at Jake. Disbelief widened her eyes. "I don't believe this!" she gasped. "I don't believe it!"

Kelly stared sightlessly out her office window. Two months . . . two long, lonely months without Sam Tyler's familiar teasing presence, his laughter or his touch. His latest hastily scrawled postcard lay on her desk, smudged with what appeared to be oil or grease. She had kept touch with progress on the blowout through the office of Boots and Coots at Port Neches, Texas. The Houston papers had run several pictures of the belching, fiery monster sitting off the Venezuelan coast. It was being touted as the worst blowout in the history of oil well firefighting. Even worse than the Devil's Cigarette Lighter in Gassi Touil in the Sahara. Already five Venezuelans had died.

Brow furrowed, Kelly turned and stared down at the postcard. I love you, Sam Tyler. Dammit, I want to see you! I don't want to wait any longer! Her nostrils flared with frustration. There was no phone where Sam Tyler was working. And certainly, no mailing address.

"Dammit!" she whispered, beginning to pace the length of her office. She worried about him. He had come off one exhausting fire only to turn around and battle this monster in the waters of the Caribbean. Was he getting enough sleep? Blowouts were no place to be caught off guard due to exhaustion. Thus far, no one from Boots and Coots company had been injured. They were known for their safety record and had never lost a man to a blowout.

She picked up his postcard, staring at the signature. He had signed it, "Love, Sam." In the two months that had passed since she had last seen him, Kelly had had time to examine her feelings for Sam. Pursing her full lips, she made a decision and buzzed her secretary.

Sam stood on the bow of the barge, legs spread apart to ride the motion of the waves lapping around them. His eyes were narrowed against the fiery sunset on the ocean in front of them. Cupping his hands to shade his eyes, he gazed at the wrecked oil platform. Coots stood beside him, a pair of binoculars in hand, watching in silence.

"That's one mean blowout," Coots finally growled, lowering the binoculars and casting a glance in Sam's direction. "Come on, let's get ashore and eat. We'll set the explosives tomorrow morning."

Sam nodded, wiping his face clean of the ever present sweat. "I think if I have frijoles and rice one more night, I'm going to die."

Coots grinned. "Hey, don't you know this is heroic work we're performing?"

Tyler snorted, walking aft with Coots. "Yeah, that's what everybody else thinks, but they aren't here in our boots."

"Stuff the heroics. I just want to get back to Houston."

Sam agreed, sitting down on a coil of rope at the rear of the boat. He rested his arms wearily on his knees, staring blankly off into the distance. Home. And Kelly. Damn, he missed her. Had she gotten the letters? The mail was undependable in this part of the world. He had signed the last one with love. If Kelly had gotten it, had she noticed that? He cradled his head wearily on his arms, exhaustion robbing him of his normal vitality. Was she taking care of herself? And had she fully recovered from her brush with death in the desert? Knowing her as he did, he guessed that she was driving everyone with a bullwhip in her effort to get her father's company back into shape. A smile edged his mouth. At least Blanchard Pipe was performing like a champ at this damn blowout. Kelly would be happy about that.

"Well I'll be," Coots rumbled. He nudged Sam on the shoulder. "Hey! You'd better see what's waiting for you on the dock, Sam. Take a look."

Sam lifted his head. It was dusk, and the fading light made those on shore look like shadows. No . . . it couldn't be . . . He stood, his eyes narrowing. His heart pounded with the tumult of emotions that surged through his body. "Kelly!" he breathed softly.

Coots grinned. "And in our white uniform! I wonder if she's ready to sign up for this blowout? God knows, we could use some Irish luck." He slapped Tyler on his broad shoulder. "She's some kind of woman! Treat her right, Sam. She's one in a million!"

Sam couldn't tear his gaze from her. "You bet she is," he agreed fervently. She stood there at the end of the dock in the white company uniform, her red hair a delicious contrast to the clothing. He could barely contain his happiness. A grin pulled at his mouth as he made eye contact with Kelly. The smile that blossomed on her face filled his heart with undeniable love for her.

The boat came alongside the dock and Sam leaped the last three feet, landing like a cat on the rickety wooden surface. Kelly's eyes were wide as she stared up at him. He closed the last few feet and opened his arms to her.

"Come here," he whispered roughly.

"Oh, Sam!" she cried, flinging her arms around his neck. He smelled of oil and sweat, but she didn't care. Hungrily, she lifted her face, meeting his descending mouth with utter abandon. He tasted of ocean salt, and his mouth was strong and masculine. A small cry of joy rose in her throat and she pressed herself shamelessly to him, luxuriating in the feel of his athletically muscled body. His hands seared her flesh as he ran them down her back, capturing her hips against him, making her aware of his need for her.

Breathlessly, she broke free of his dizzying kiss. Kelly cradled his face between her slender fingers, anxiously searching his eyes. "You look awful!" she wailed. He had a two-day growth of beard, his cheeks were gaunt from not eating properly and his eyes were red-rimmed.

Sam lifted her off her feet as if she were a feather, crushing her in his embrace, ignoring her protest. "God, how I've missed you, woman," he whispered hoarsely against her hair.

She struggled free. "I was right! You were sick! Oh, Sam, why didn't you come home?"

He laughed, bringing her back into his arms. "I'm not sick, my redhaired witch. This always happens on a long haul with a blowout of this sort." His blue eyes crinkled with warmth. "You look absolutely beautiful, Kelly Blanchard. Just what the hell are you doing down here? Did you get a yellow fever vaccination? A cholera shot before you came?"

Tears welled up in her eyes. His voice was laden with emotion. She couldn't—wouldn't keep her hands off him. "Of course I did!"

He placed his arm around her shoulders, guiding her down the dock. In all directions men, machinery and trucks swarmed over the jungle landscape. Kelly turned, catching a glimpse of the oil platform burning fiercely offshore. She glanced up at Sam.

"You look terrible. Haven't they been giving you enough rest?"

He gave her a crooked grin. "You keep telling me how bad I look, woman."

"Sam Tyler, I'm mentioning it because I care, dammit!"

"That's more like it." He gave her a pat on the rear. "Come on, we got beans and rice to look forward to for dinner tonight."

Kelly shook her head. "No you don't. I brought down a care package of good Texas beef steaks, corn on the cob and beer."

Sam laughed. "You're one incredible woman, honey. Come on, I'm starved!"

The men of the company gathered in the dingy shack that they called home when they weren't fighting the blowout. Coots rewarded Kelly with a huge smile when the Venezuelan cook brought out the medium-rare steaks on a huge platter. They sat squeezed around the table, elbows and knees touching. The laughter, jokes and merriment were unchecked. Kelly took great pleasure in watching Sam consume his meal.

"Is Houston the same without us?" Coots wanted to know, finishing up the last of the steak.

Kelly shook her head. "We're all pining away for you boys."

"Man," Colly growled, "I want to get home. Two blowouts back to back is enough to kill ya."

Sam nodded his agreement and took a swig of the cold beer. He handed it to Kelly, who took a sip. "Another two days and we ought to be ready to fly out, Colly. Hang in there, buddy."

"Two days?" Kelly asked, a hopeful note in her voice.

"Yep," Coots said, rising. "Now that we got all the debris off the deck, we're placing the explosives over the fire tomorrow. The platform was a mangled mess when we arrived."

Sam rose, pulling Kelly with him. "Enough shoptalk. You guys excuse me while I take my best girl for a walk."

The evening air was damp with the smell of the jungle mixed with the tangy salt air from the Caribbean. The stars were coming out, glittering like cut crystals in the black heavens above them. Kelly was content to lay her head on his shoulder as they walked slowly down a well-trodden path toward the shore.

"Your girl, huh?"

"Yup. You got any objections?"

"Yes, as a matter of fact, I do."

Sam raised one eyebrow and stopped, resting his arms on her shoulders as she faced him. The shadows moved across his craggy face, the lantern light defining his strong, sensual mouth and jawline. "You're mighty spirited tonight, Kelly Blanchard. I've been trying to piece together why you came down here."

Her heart took a leap. "I won't play games with you, Sam." She swallowed hard, forcing the words out, afraid of the consequences. "I was lonely in Houston by myself."

He tilted his head. "The prettiest woman in Houston lonely? Come on. How many single millionaires have come to your door since you got back from the Sahara?"

"I turned them all down."

"Oh?"

"Yes." Her green eyes became more serious as she met his stare.

"Why did you come down here?" he repeated, running his callused hands lightly over her back.

"You know why."

Sam feigned innocence. "Was it to see if Blanchard Pipe was standing up to the rigors of the job?"

Kelly clenched her teeth. "You haven't changed one bit, Sam Tyler! And get that self-satisfied look off your face! Oh!" She spun on her heel, walking at a fast pace back toward the camp.

Sam's laughter was soft, disturbing. In an instant, he had captured her arm and swung her around. "And you haven't changed one iota either. Now come here and quit fighting me."

Kelly struggled as he placed both arms around her, drawing her against the hard planes of his body. His blue eyes were alive with laughter as he watched her settle down. "That's better," he praised, kissing her flaming red hair. "I can see that two months without me around hasn't improved your mood any. I wonder why that is?" he whispered. He kissed her earlobe and then her temple. "I've missed you," he growled softly.

"Sam," she protested weakly, "I didn't come down here just to . . ."

"No man in his right mind would think of you as just a bedwarmer," he murmured.

Kelly wanted to erase that maddening smile that lingered on his wonderful mouth. Her intuition told her Sam knew why she had flown down here and it galled her to think he wasn't taking her seriously. Weakly, she placed her hands against his chest, trying to push him away.

"Sam, quit making this tougher than it already is!"

He sobered. "I'm sorry, Kelly." He offered her a slight smile and brushed her cheek with the back of his hand. "I know why you came down," he provided softly.

Kelly gave him a startled glance. "You do?" Her voice sounded high, off-key.

"My postcard."

She blinked. "Postcard?" she echoed.

"Yes, the postcard."

She blinked once. "I—"

"I signed it 'love.' Remember?"

"Oh . . . of course . . ."

He placed his hand beneath her chin. "Come on, we've got to talk."

She followed him wordlessly down the narrow path until it widened onto a small stretch of beach. As they sat down, Kelly suddenly felt very afraid. She had been such a fool to come down here!

"I'm glad you came," Sam said, holding her hands.

"Now I'm not so sure," she muttered, unable to meet his gaze.

"What's the matter, getting cold feet?" he baited gently.

Kelly grimaced. "I've made a complete fool out of myself . . ."

"I don't think so." His grip was warm and strong. "Matter of fact, I admire your courage, Kelly. I want to know that the woman I marry isn't afraid of life. I want her to be brave and adventurous, with a dash of reckless- ness thrown in just for spice."

"You do . . . ?"

He nodded. "I made a promise to myself after my first marriage, Kelly. I made a mistake in marrying a woman who saw me as her sole emotional support. And after the divorce, I knew I needed just the opposite. I need a woman who is in charge of herself. Who is strong like me. That way, when I have a weak moment, I can lean on her. I'm not always strong. And I don't expect my wife to always be either. What about you? What do you expect of the man you want to marry?"

She lowered her gaze. "I . . . I learned from Todd that I didn't need a man who was going to try to destroy me." She frowned, the words coming slowly. "I want a man who will love me for exactly what I am instead of what I'm not. Does that make sense?"

"Perfect sense. What took you so long to get down here, Kelly Blanchard?"

Kelly gave him a startled look. "What?"

Sam forced himself to remain serious. "I expected you to come down here sooner and propose to me."

Her lips parted, her eyes widened in shock. "Why . . . you . . ." She jerked her hands out of his and scrambled to her feet. "You're such a—"

Sam was on his feet as quickly as a cat. Before she could say another word he growled, "Marry me."

"What—"

"I said, marry me," Sam reiterated.

Her anger abated as she stared up at him. "You meant to ask me all along, Sam Tyler!" she accused.

His smile widened. "Yes, I did."

"You're impossible!" she protested.

"And I love you," he murmured near her ear. "Do you love me enough to be known as Kelly Blanchard-Tyler?"

Her emerald eyes sparkled. "At least you were wise enough to leave the Blanchard in. It proves you're not a total male chauvinist, Sam Tyler. And it also shows your sensitivity."

He nodded. "Guilty on all counts." He imprisoned her face between his hands. "Now," he breathed, "will you be my wife, my best friend and my lover for the rest of our lives?"

Tears welled in her eyes and she touched his cheek.

"Yes . . . yes, I will. Oh, Sam! I love you so much!" she exclaimed, throwing herself against him.

It was as if they were back on the Rub al Khali Desert when it came to sleeping arrangements. The porta-camp had been set up just inside the jungle treeline to afford some protection from the blazing tropic sun during the day. Sam kept his arm around her waist as they walked silently back toward the camp.

"There's even less room to sleep in the shack this time," Sam warned.

"I'm getting used to this kind of lifestyle, Sam Tyler."

He managed a wry grin. "As much as I want to make love to you, it's out of the question."

Kelly looked up at his shadowed face. "I know. And it's all right. I'm not marrying you just because you make wonderful love with me."

His hand tightened around her momentarily. "You aren't so bad yourself, my redheaded witch," he said huskily, dropping a kiss on her hair. "We've got one cot left. Let me rearrange things and I'll put you in the room we use for storing our supplies."

The exhausted men were already sleeping, so Kelly made sure she moved silently through the sleeping quarters. Sam set up the cot, found a lightweight blanket and turned off the light. He came over and pulled Kelly back into his arms.

"I love you," he whispered.

She made a small, throaty sound as she sought his mouth. The kiss was gentle and exploring. Hungrily, Kelly drank of his strength, pressing her lips more firmly to his mouth. She felt Sam tremble, felt his arms tighten around her in powerful reaction. Her heartbeat rose as his tongue masterfully invaded her with delectable ease. Her breasts grew taut, the nipples hardening against the material of her coveralls.

Slowly, Sam pulled her away from him. She was quivering, her eyes burning with an unquenchable desire. He took a deep breath.

"Get some sleep," he said thickly.

Kelly grimaced. "That's a laugh," she whispered breathlessly.

Amusement lingered in his eyes. "For both of us," Sam agreed. "I'll see you tomorrow morning, honey. Dream of us."

Kelly awoke at dawn when Coots and the team began moving around. She dressed quickly and met them out in the makeshift kitchen. The smell of freshly perked coffee filled the cramped space and it smelled like heaven to her. Coots offered her a dented aluminum mug.

She took a chair and sat at Coots's elbow. "What will you do today?"

"We're gonna put the explosives in a fifty-gallon drum and wrap it in a fire retardant material. Then we'll get a crane positioned on the lip of the platform to place the explosives in the fire. Tomorrow we'll actually place the drum in the fire and detonate it." Frowning, Coots took another swallow of coffee. "The explosion will deprive the fire of oxygen long enough for it to extinguish itself."

Colly rubbed his lean, Texan face wearily. "Providing those damn winds don't change on us again."

Kelly looked at the mechanic. "What will happen if they do?"

Colly drew out a pencil and drew a quick sketch on a piece of paper. "We got five water monitors set up on three barges anchored around the platform. Every time the wind changes direction or blows too hard the barges are torn from their positions and then we have to reposition them on the leeward side of the platform and set everything back up again." He tapped the scribbled drawing. "It's critical that we have enough water pouring on that fire when we use the explosives. The metal on that pipe at the core of the blowout is superheated. The explosion will momentarily deprive the fire of oxygen and it'll extinguish itself. But it can reignite seconds after that if the water isn't there to keep the metal pipe cool enough to prevent it from firing up again."

Sam wandered in and glanced over at the table. "Those winds will remain the same, Colly," he said, reaching for a cup and pouring himself coffee.

Colly gave him a questioning look. "Oh yeah? Did the good fairy tell you that last night?"

Sam sat opposite Kelly and gave her a warm look. She looked absolutely ravishing this morning, he thought. Her red hair was slightly curled from the humidity and her eyes sparkled. He wanted to lose himself in them. Colly was still staring at him and Sam roused himself from those pleasant thoughts to answer his question.

"No. Our luck's changed," he said. "We've got our Irish luck now. We won't have to move those barges around as we've been having to do every third day or so."

Colly grinned over at Kelly. "You realize Sam's making you the scapegoat in all this?"

Kelly tore her gaze from Sam's face. Despite his exhaustion he looked incredibly virile and masculine. There was a flame of happiness glimmering in the depths of his azure eyes. She was responsible for that joy and

Kelly felt an undeniable thrill. A smile crossed her lips. "There's only one thing better than Texas luck, Colly, and that's Irish luck. Didn't everything go smoothly over in Saudi Arabia when I was there?"

Colly grinned. "Oh sure. You got kidnapped and almost raped. And then we didn't think you were going to pull through for a couple days in the hospital."

She shrugged. "I mean at the blowout. Don't worry about me."

"Yeah, the blowout went smooth. Real smooth."

Kelly tilted her head, laughing. "And things will go smoothly from here on out."

Sam slowly rose to get a second cup of coffee. "Lady luck's on our side, men."

11

꧁◦◦◦◦◦◦◦◦◦◦꧂

Kelly stood at the end of the dock with a pair of binoculars raised to her eyes. Because of the dangers involved, Coots didn't want her on the barge assembly. They had spent all morning on the dock lining a fifty-gallon drum with shock absorbent material and asbestos. Then they placed the dynamite inside and sealed it securely. Afterward, the drum had been wrapped in more asbestos and then a foillike material to reflect the extreme heat of the flames. If the dynamite inside the drum got too hot, it would explode before they were able to use the crane hook to position it properly. And if that happened, the men who were perched on that platform crane could be killed outright or severely injured by the untimely blast.

The hot sun bore down on her and the humidity was high. The coveralls clung to her damp skin. Lowering the binoculars, Kelly walked back toward the camp. She didn't need to invite another case of heat exhaustion and end up in the hospital again. It looked as though the men had almost completed the positioning of the crane hook.

Kelly looked longingly at the small cove a quarter of a mile from the dock. Luckily, there was no oil spill from the damaged platform and the water was clear and inviting. It was a lot better than the desert, Kelly thought. Making up her mind, she walked quickly back to the camp.

After changing into a pale lime-colored bathing suit, Kelly wasted little time grabbing a towel she had unpacked from her suitcase and walking down to the secluded cove. In the distance, only the orange and yellow flame broke the beauty of the horizon. All around her birds in brilliant colors sang melodically. The verdant green of the jungle trees added to the loveliness of the setting.

After making sure the sandy shelf of the cove did not suddenly drop off into deep water, Kelly sank into the welcoming depths. The water slid over her, warm, salty and refreshing. Her hair became a darkened mass, flowing like a copper sheet across her shoulders as she swam. Kelly lost track of time, immersed in the soothing water that shielded her from the overpowering tropic heat.

She had rolled onto her back, simply floating with her eyes closed. The lapping of water on the shore was suddenly punctuated by a splashing noise. Concerned, Kelly opened her eyes and rolled onto her stomach. Her eyes widened in surprise as she saw Sam swimming toward her.

He moved cleanly through the water, the muscles of his arms and shoulders glistening. Her lips parted in unconscious reaction as he neared and she swam forward to meet him. He drew her daringly against him, pressing his mouth to her lips.

She tasted salt in his kiss as she responded to his invitation. The lapping of the water, the sliding friction of their bodies against one another increased her pleasure. Hungrily, she returned the ardor of his lips, eager to take advantage of this stolen, unexpected moment.

Sam broke away, his blue eyes disturbingly dark with desire. He smoothed the hair from her cheek.

"You look like a beautiful mermaid," he said huskily.

Kelly smiled. "Thank you. You look kind of delicious yourself," she replied, running her fingers down his shoulders and across the powerful breadth of his chest.

"Watch it," he growled, gripping her by the waist. "That could be dangerous. . . ."

Her lilting laughter heightened the swirling tension between them as they treaded water. "I'm used to living with danger, Sam Tyler," she challenged.

"Yeah?"

"Yeah."

He grinned, curving his arm around her waist and then swimming toward shore. "Okay, let's live dangerously, then," he said.

She gave him a startled look. "But . . . what about the others?"

"I thought you said you liked to live dangerously."

They touched the bottom of the cove and Kelly steadied herself against Sam as they waded out of the water. Her hair hung in burnished sheets, framing her face; her green eyes were brilliant with happiness. "I do . . . but I like to take some precautions."

Sam laughed heartily, scooping her up into his arms

and carrying her to the sandy beach. A blanket had already been spread beneath the shade provided by the trees, and he gently deposited her upon it. A mischievous smile lingered on his strong, sensual mouth as he rested above her, preventing her escape.

"Now the lady has reservations. Really, I thought you were fearless," he taunted.

Kelly's caution gave way to his teasing good humor. He looked incredibly virile. In the dappled sunlight his hair lay plastered and gleaming against his skull. The dark mat of hair on his chest was beginning to curl. "When I have to be," she laughed, running her fingertips lightly across his chest.

Sam's eyes grew dark as he studied her. Water dripped off his square jaw. "Now you have to be," he growled in warning.

"I've never backed down from anything yet," she whispered, slipping her arm around his neck and drawing him down upon her.

Sam gently caressed her lips, tasting them, outlining them, coaxing her to react to his provocation. She moaned, pressing her body against the hard length of his, deepening the exploratory kiss. He slid the straps of her bathing suit off her shoulders, slowly pulling it downward to free her beautifully rounded breasts. He deepened the kiss, caressing her, taunting the nipples into yearning hardness. A moan escaped from her and he felt her breathing change, becoming shallower with need.

"My redhaired witch," he growled softly against lips that were glistening petals of pale pink. Her eyes were an emerald green flecked with the gold of desire. Tendrils of copper-colored hair curled around her face. He watched as each touch of his hand drove her closer and closer to the edge of sheer ecstasy. Her lashes swept downward against her cheeks as he caressed the length of her body. This time, there would be no hurry, no need to rush. Now they could savor one another fully.

He eased the suit off her and marveled at the supple beauty of her body. Her skin was ivory and velvet, tightening wherever he slid his callused fingers. Leaning down, Sam captured a nipple, pulled on it gently, and heard her moan with pleasure. Urgently, she pressed her body against him, demanding more of him. All of him. Shedding his bathing trunks, Sam lay back down, and pulled her on top of him. Her dark red hair tumbled across her shoulders. He nuzzled her slender neck, placing a series of kisses across her collarbone until he reached her taut breast.

Her fingernails dug convulsively into his shoulders. A small cry of pleasure erupted from her throat as he gently guided her upon him. She froze for a moment, esctasy written on her features, her body taut. He groaned, feeling the warmth of her love, barely able to control himself as he allowed her those precious moments to adjust to him. Her lashes lifted and her green eyes burned with the fierce gold of unrestrained passion as she met his gaze. He reached up, bringing her face down so he could kiss her lips. "Love me," he whispered against her lips. "And let me love you. . . ." She barely nodded, before finding his mouth once more and pressing her body down against him.

Sam groaned, clutching her slim hips, moving in rhythm to needs that had been restrained too long. She was an incredible creature, moving with effortless grace. Moments fled into an eternity of heightening pleasure. He felt her tense and saw the beauty of esctasy crossing her mobile features. A cry of pleasure echoed from her throat and he held her tightly to him, reveling with her in the joy of the release. Moments later, he joined her celebration of love. She fell against him and lay there breathing hard, exhausted.

The warm wind lightly rippled the surface of the water in the cove. Kelly barely roused herself, content to hear the steady beat of Sam's heart against her ear. Her hair was nearly dry now as she raised her head, resting her chin on his chest. Drowsy blue eyes met hers.

"I love you, Sam Tyler," she murmured huskily, reaching out and tracing his brow.

He gave her a gentle pat on the rear with his left hand. "It's mutual, believe me." He closed his eyes. "Has anybody ever told you that you're one hell of a woman?" His words sent a quiver of joy through her.

"Just you. But then, that's all that counts, isn't it?"

Sam opened one eye. God, she looked like a dream come to life. The sun had changed position, its light cascading through the leaves to strike her hair with fiery golden highlights. He placed both hands on her shoulders, then ran them down the length of her back until they came to rest on her hips. "I've missed you, honey."

Tears sprang unexpectedly to her eyes as she heard the loneliness in his tone. She rested on his chest, watching the water lap, lap, lap at the edge of the cove. "It's been terrible without you, Sam," she admitted, a quaver in her voice.

He frowned when he saw the path of tears down her cheeks. Carefully brushing her face dry, he asked, "How terrible?"

Kelly groaned, avoiding his eyes. "Forget it," she said, "I don't want to talk about it now."

"No you don't," he admonished. "You're upset about something. What is it?"

She shrugged. "We've just made the most beautiful love I've ever experienced and you want to talk!"

Sam grinned good-naturedly, running his fingers through her silken hair. "When I hear that kind of catch in your voice, yes, I do. Now, let's hear it."

Kelly remonstrated with herself for allowing company problems to crop up between them. And yet, Sam was being patient with her. Todd had not been like that at all. How many times had she wanted to discuss her deepest fears or personal feelings after lovemaking? She gazed up into Sam's face, realizing that he wasn't like Todd in any respect. "You really don't mind?"

"If I did, I'd tell you so." He got up and retrieved their bathing suits. "Let's get these on before the guys come down here for their evening bath," he suggested. "Then we can talk."

Her suit was almost dry and Kelly slipped it back on, returning to his arms afterward. She rested her head on his shoulder, content as never before. Sam placed a kiss on her hair.

"Okay, what's been happening since I left Houston?" he asked.

Her green eyes darkened and she grimaced. "When I got to the office, Sam, I found out more about our pipe problems."

"Such as?"

"The formula given to R & B Steel had not been followed."

Sam nuzzled her hair. "Your father's formula, right?"

"Yes." She felt new anger stirring in her, chasing away

the euphoric feeling she had experienced moments ago. "Jake hired a detective in Pittsburgh to find out why the pipe was failing. Apparently, someone bribed the metallurgist over at R and B."

Sam rubbed his jaw. "Who?"

"He refused to tell us, but I have my suspicions," she ground out.

"Gage Wallace," Sam stated with certainty.

She nodded. "I can't prove it. Not yet. But Wallace is supposed to be in Houston on Friday. I told him I wanted to see him."

Sam disengaged his arm from around her shoulders and sat opposite her on the blanket. His brows were drawn down, eyes narrowed with thought. "If he did do it, he'd never admit it, honey."

She flashed him an angry glance. "Maybe . . . maybe not. I don't know. All I do know is that I'll handle that confrontation at the time. I want to see where he's coming from. Maybe I can manuever him into admitting it. I don't know."

Sam picked up her hand. "And if you can?"

"I've already started working with our attorneys to take the case to R and B Steel to have them pay damages. But if I can get Wallace to make an admission, I'll slap him with a lawsuit that will ruin him once and for all."

He nodded. "That means you'll have to leave tomorrow, then."

Kelly agreed, morose. "I know. But it was worth the quick trip down here. I just couldn't stand it any longer, Sam. I had to see you." She gave an embarrassed shrug. "I never thought I'd say that to another man again."

Sam whispered her name, pulling her back into his arms, loving her fiery spirit, her courage and her honesty. "You're off on your charger to tilt at another windmill," he teased gently, kissing her cheek.

Kelly wrapped her arms around his naked waist, just content to spend this quiet time with him. "I'm doing it for my father, Sam," she said softly. "Dad never cheated anyone in his whole life. He had a wonderful reputation in the oil and gas industry until Wallace got into the act." She closed her eyes, a sudden wave of sadness passing through her. "I feel like a vengeful angel right now," she admitted. "I want to get Wallace. I want to hurt him like he hurt my father."

Sam embraced her for a long, long time. He simply rocked her, aware of her anguish. Nothing could take that away. Only an attempt to rectify the situation could help. Finally, he released her, pulling her upward and into his arms as he stood. Placing a feathery kiss on her lips, he whispered, "Just remember, I love you, Kelly Blanchard. And I love your courage in the face of adversity." His eyes narrowed upon her upturned features. "I just wish I could be there for that confrontation."

She shook her head. "It's just as well you aren't, Sam. You two get along like two dogs in a fight," she said ruefully, a glimmer of a smile in her eyes.

The sun was barely edging the horizon the next morning when the barge carrying the drum of explosives chugged away from the dock. Kelly stood, her lips still tingling from the kiss Sam had given her before boarding the barge. Cupping her hands to her eyes, she watched them make headway toward the burning oil platform in the distance. Just as Sam had promised, the wind had remained slight, so they wouldn't have to change the positions of the water monitors or barges.

Her heart rose in her throat as she watched them near the mangled platform. She had barely slept last night, wanting to be in Sam's arms and not on the cot by herself. Finally, she had found a man whom she could respect and lean on. And just as important, a man who could lean on her in times of need. A wry smile crossed her mouth. And hadn't she sworn she would never marry again? Sam was different. He was more sensitive than any man she had ever met. She wondered how Todd would react to her trying to trap Gage Wallace. Disgust tinged her jade green eyes. Todd would have said it was beyond the scope of a woman to play rough in the world of business and survive.

Taking a deep breath, she picked up the binoculars. Kelly spotted four men in white coveralls climbing a ladder up to the deck of the blackened platform. All the debris had been cleared away with cranes and hooks. The only thing that remained on the scorched deck was a huge candle-shaped flame roaring three hundred and fifty feet skyward. Several galvanized shields were standing near the base of the flame, protecting the men of Boots and Coots as they worked with swift precision. The heavy water spray from the monitors blotted out the details of what they were doing and Kelly felt a twinge of momentary terror. What if they couldn't maneuver that drum into the flame in time? It would explode, destroying the hook and crane assembly as well as anything else in the vicinity.

Be careful, she told Sam silently. She recalled his fiery

touch, his mouth upon her lips and the wild abandon that he aroused in her when they made love. She would never tire of his touch . . . of his love. She lowered the glasses, realizing it would take another hour before they would be ready to hoist the drum containing the explosives. Walking back to the end of the dock, she sat on the sandy beach. Worry kept nagging at her as she watched the blowout roaring in the distance. Her life had been like that flame since her divorce—out of control, without constructive purpose. And just now, her life was gaining meaning again. Compressing her lips, Kelly tried to stop worrying about Sam's safety. Would she always feel like this when he had to go out on a job? Or would she eventually get used to it?

Not likely, she decided. Every blowout was difficult; sometimes untried, innovative techniques had to be used to cap and extinguish the blaze. But Sam loved this life as much as she loved running a corporation. There was challenge in it for both of them in different ways. And unlike Todd, Sam would give her a free hand in running her company the way she saw fit. Kelly loved him fiercely. He would be there if she needed him, her team partner. And she would be there for him.

"Hurry," she whispered, getting back to her feet. "Hurry up and kill that flame."

She didn't have long to wait. The crew clambered back to the crane on the edge of the rigging platform after loading the drum on the hook assembly. From the safety of the barge, the crane operator, Colly, began to lift the drum containing the explosives. They only had two to three minutes to place the drum at the base of the flame before it would ignite in the intense temperature of the surrounding fire. Every water monitor was fixed on the platform, spraying thousands of gallons of sea water upon the flame.

Kelly didn't know what to expect when the drum exploded. Colly expertly placed it into the flame. Seconds later she saw huge balls of fire shooting skyward. The thundering explosion seemed to tear the world apart. Unprepared, she pressed her hands against her ears, wincing as the sound boomed on like someone pounding kettledrums next to her. She flinched, closing her eyes reflexively. When she opened them, she saw that the flame was out! The monitors continued to pour sea water onto the platform, and steam rose in huge, billowing clouds from the area surrounding the blowout. Clasping her hands to her heart, she realized that the flame would remain extinguished. Sam was safe! And soon, he would be home!

Gage entered Kelly Blanchard's office with a suave smile on his mouth. He was impeccably dressed in a three-piece suit which subtly reminded everyone of his financial success. He saw her standing with her back to the window, her fiery red hair arranged in a Gibson girl. He raised an eyebrow. He liked the hairdo on Kelly. The tendrils softened her features, giving her a decidedly vulnerable look. The apricot-colored dress brought out the pink in her cheeks and the emerald color of her eyes.

"You look beautiful today, Kelly," he greeted, coming over and picking up her hand, placing a kiss on it.

She gave him a cool, measuring smile, withdrawing her fingers. "Thank you, Gage. Please, have a seat."

He walked to the leather chair opposite her own and

casually sat down. His brown eyes narrowed upon her. "Word's gotten around that you had a close call over in Saudi Arabia."

Kelly met his gaze with a slight smile. "You know me, Gage. I'm always in hot water of some kind."

He laughed softly. "Yes, you always were bent upon self-destruction of some sort."

"I don't call living life self-destruction."

"Todd saw it that way."

"I'm not married to Todd anymore, so it's a moot point, isn't it?"

Gage crossed his legs. "More to the point, did Blanchard pipe stand up to the stress of the desert test?"

Kelly swallowed her building anger, watching him closely. "Yes, it did stand up to the demands placed upon it. Why do you ask?"

"Just because of the gossip going around the industry about Blanchard Pipe."

"Yes, I'm aware of it." She leaned forward on her elbows, forcing a sweet smile and hating every second of it. "Tell me, Gage, what do you think I should do about it?"

"Honestly?"

"Have you ever been less than that with me?" Oh, God, she could barely stand herself. Wallace actually thought she was as dumb as she was acting.

"Of course not, Kelly." He smiled broadly. "You know I've always had your best interests at heart." He got up, pacing slowly, keeping his gaze upon her. "And speaking of heart . . ." He stopped, turning fully upon her. "My offer still stands. I think matrimony would be an excellent political move for you."

Bile rose in her throat and Kelly had to forcefully stop herself from releasing the tight rein on her temper. She swallowed hard. "I'm more concerned at the moment about my father's formula. R and B Steel didn't mix it correctly and that's why that one batch of pipe blew."

Wallace's brown eyes lightened considerably and he stepped over to her desk. "Kelly, you know my steel company would mix the formula for you. I'd give you a fair deal." He shrugged. "You can't stand another bad batch mixed up, you know . . ." he drawled.

She got up, walking to the window, her back to him. Why had she thought she could carry off this confrontation? He was acting as if he were completely innocent. Crossing her arms, she turned on her heel to face him. "You've been wanting our business for a long time, Gage."

"True. What steel company wouldn't?"

Her green eyes narrowed. "Tell me," she began lightly, "do you know Mark Hamilton?"

Wallace didn't blink. "Who?"

Her heart beat more quickly. "Mark Hamilton, the metallurgist over at R and B Steel."

He pursed his lips. "No . . . although I've heard the name somewhere."

I'll bet you have, Kelly thought savagely. She walked determinedly back over to her desk, glancing at the intercom, which had purposely been left in the "open" position. In her secretary's office was Detective Barbara Whiting. The Houston policewoman was there to listen, record and bear witness to Wallace's confession. *If* she could get him to confess.

"You claim you don't know Hamilton," she snapped.

"Then why the hell does he say you paid him twenty-five thousand dollars to spoil our formula?"

Wallace's eyes showed momentary surprise. He raised his chin, his lips thinning. "I underestimated you, Kelly."

She gave him an icy smile, her eyes glittering like green shards of glass. "Completely."

"You realize you can't prove a thing, my dear. I'll admit to you that I paid off Hamilton. But I'll swear just the opposite if you try to take this to court. It'll be my word against Hamilton's."

Kelly remained frozen for fear of her temper exploding. Her voice was low, quavering. "This is one time when you don't have all the cards in the poker game, Wallace. This entire conversation has been taped. Detective Whiting, you may come in now and read Mr. Wallace his rights."

Shock registered on Wallace's drawn features. "Give a woman a company to run and she thinks she can play with the big boys." He exploded into a bitter laugh, watching as a tall, brunette woman in civilian clothes entered the office.

The adrenaline that had been pounding through Kelly's veins was making her shaky. Relief coursed through her and she took a deep breath. "You never did think a woman could make it in a man's world, Gage."

Wallace saw the detective open her badge case to prove her identity to him. He twisted his head toward Kelly. "You've got the fight of your life on your hands, Ms. Blanchard. My attorneys will still get me off. You'll see."

Kelly's eyes flashed fire. "The evidence is already in."

She gave him a fixed smile. "Hamilton never would admit who paid him off. But your confession makes that unnecessary. And it was a woman who was your undoing. I think I'm going to get as much satisfaction out of this as you did trying to destroy Blanchard Pipe for your own selfish ends."

"Mr. Wallace? I'm Detective Whiting of the Houston Police Department and I'm placing you under arrest. You have the right to remain silent . . ."

It was over. Wallace stood there stonily as the detective read him his rights. With one last venomous glance, he left her office. Words weren't necessary, Kelly thought, collapsing in her chair. Tears streamed down her cheeks. It would be a long and costly court battle, but she didn't care. It was the only way to salvage her father's name in an industry where a gentleman's agreement was still respected and sealed with a handshake. Wiping the tears away with the back of her hand, she looked over at the calendar. If only Sam were home . . . But it would take another four days to load the equipment and fly it back Stateside. Right now, her emotions were stripped and raw. Kelly craved his closeness and the silent support he always gave her by simply being there. This was a battle she had to fight for herself, she realized. And fight she would. "At least I didn't lose my temper," she groused, blotting her eyes once again.

Going to the washroom, Kelly repaired her makeup and put a touch of lipstick on for good measure to bolster her bruised ego. The day was only half over, she realized. And it was almost noon. Today she needed a drink. The idea was a tantalizing reprieve and she went to her office, grabbing her purse.

"Where do you think you're going?"

Kelly swallowed a gasp. Her eyes widened. "Sam!" she cried, throwing her arms around his neck.

He grinned, pulling her against him, loving the feel of her soft curves against his body. He inhaled deeply of her warm scent. "God, you smell good," he whispered, burying his face against her hair, "like fresh apricots. And you look beautiful."

Stunned at his appearance, she could only hug him tightly. "Oh, Sam . . . I'm so glad you're home! So glad. . . ."

"Hey . . . tears?" He released her, cupping her chin and forcing her to meet his gaze. "Of happiness, I hope?" he teased.

"Yes . . . no . . . oh, I just had that meeting with Wallace," she blurted. "Don't mind me, I'm just a big crybaby."

Sam chuckled softly, pulling a clean handkerchief from the pocket of his white uniform. "I happen to love a certain big crybaby. Now stand still for just a moment and let me wipe the tears away."

Kelly stood obediently, her heart thumping wildly in her breast. She blinked several times, searching his face. He was freshly showered and clean shaven. His uniform was white and fresh. "When did you get in? I mean—"

He dropped a kiss on her lips, effectively silencing her. She tasted sweet, clean and inviting as he explored her responsive lips. Finally, he drew away, his eyes turbulent with awakening desire. "I talked Coots into letting me come home early. I didn't want you facing Wallace alone," he explained.

Kelly's face grew tender. "Oh, Sam . . ."

"Looks like I was a little late."

She leaned against him, slipping her arms around his waist, content to be held by him. "No, you're never too late."

"Were you able to make him admit his part in the bribery?"

"Yes, but it was a terrible scene."

Sam nodded. "Now it means a court battle."

"Yes. Wallace is running scared, Sam. And it's about time."

He gave her a brief hug. "Come on, let's talk over the details at lunch. Hungry?" There was mirth in the depths of his blue eyes as he gazed down at her.

She gave him one fierce embrace and then slipped her hand into his. "Starved for you, Sam Tyler."

He shared a wicked smile with her. "Then I have a better idea. You have any pressing appointments this afternoon?"

She shook her head. "What did you have in mind?"

He guided her down the hall and out to the white Cadillac with the Boots and Coots emblem on the doors. "I told Coots I was taking a few weeks off."

"Weeks?" she gasped, turning to him, her eyes wide with disbelief.

Sam's laughter was infectious as he drank in her indignant expression. "Oh, I see. The lady thinks I'm inviting her to my bed not for an afternoon but for a couple of weeks!"

She turned crimson. "You're such a—"

"There she goes again, blowing off all that Irish steam.

Accusing me of being a sex fiend when my intentions were strictly honorable." He grinned, his teeth white against the bronze of his flesh, his blue eyes crinkled with laughter. He gripped her arm. "Come on, Kelly Blanchard, let's go eat. We've got a whole lifetime of plans to discuss this afternoon."

JULY TITLES

MANDY'S SONG
Jeanne Stephens

TO LOVE A DREAMER
Ruth Langan

RENDEZVOUS
Nancy John

A WORLD OF THEIR OWN
Linda Wisdom

SILKEN THREADS
Monica Barrie

HAVEN OF TENDERNESS
Carolyn Thornton

Silhouette Desire

COMING NEXT MONTH

THE BEST REASONS
Beverly Bird

Sabrina Caide ran the marina on Thunder Cay, the island that was her refuge from an unhappy former life. Then Chase Cutter entered the harbor and took over her days — and her nights — forcing her back into the mainstream she sought to avoid...

CAPITOL AFFAIR
Fran Bergen

They both worked for the government in the education field, each with a lesson to teach the other. Professionally, Jeff was the key to Monica's success. Emotionally he capitalized on her deepest affections.

MORE THAN PROMISES
Amanda Lee

It all started with an unexpected phone call one blustery March morning. Laura Carson was instantly intrigued by the very masculine voice on the other end of the line. And when she met the darkly attractive Brandon McGuire, she found him even more intriguing in person.

Silhouette Desire

COMING NEXT MONTH

THE DEVIL TO PAY
Stephanie James

Emmy was desperate, and Julian could help her —
for a price. She was confident she could pay no
matter what he charged...until Julian called in her
I.O.U.

THE TENDER BARBARIAN
Dixie Browning

When Bey roared into Emily's life on his BMW
motorcycle she did her level best to eject him. She
soon realized that there was a bit of the barbarian in
everyone...and now she had one of her very own.

STARSTRUCK LOVERS
Suzanne Michelle

Gypsy Hamilton, international rock star, was light-
years away from the more cosmic variety, but she was
equally as dazzling. When she met Luke, she felt a
charge that jolted her to the tips of her toes. But would
a love as white-hot as the stars burn too bright to last?

Four New
Silhouette Romances
could be yours
ABSOLUTELY FREE

Did you know that Silhouette Romances are no longer available from the shops in the U.K?

Read on to discover how you could receive four brand new Silhouette Romances, **free** and **without obligation,** with this special introductory offer to the new Silhouette Reader Service.

As thousands of women who have read these books know — Silhouette Romances sweep you away into an exciting love filled world of fascination between men and women. A world filled with

age-old conflicts — love and money, ambition and guilt, jealousy and pride, even life and death.

Silhouette Romances are the latest stories written by the world's best romance writers, and they are **only** available from Silhouette Reader Service. Take out a subscription and you could receive 6 brand new titles every month, plus a newsletter bringing you all the latest information from Silhouette's New York editors. All this delivered in one exciting parcel direct to your door, with no charges for postage and packing.

And at only 95p for a book, Silhouette Romances represent the very best value in Romantic Reading.

Remember, Silhouette Romances are **only** available to subscribers, so don't miss out on this very special opportunity. Fill in the certificate below and post it today. You don't even need a stamp.

FREE BOOK CERTIFICATE

To: Silhouette Reader Service, FREEPOST, P.O. Box 236, Croydon, Surrey. CR9 9EL

Readers in South Africa—write to:
Silhouette Romance Club, Private Bag X3010, Randburg 2125.

Yes, please send me, free and without obligation, four brand new Silhouette Romances and reserve a subscription for me. If I decide to subscribe, I shall receive six brand new books every month for £5.70 , post and packing free. If I decide not to subscribe I shall write to you within 10 days. The free books are mine to keep, whatever I decide. I understand that I may cancel my subscription at any time simply by writing to you. I am over 18 years of age. Please write in BLOCK CAPITALS.

Signature _____

Name _____

Address _____

_____ Postcode _____

SEND NO MONEY — TAKE NO RISKS.
Please don't forget to include your Postcode.

Remember postcodes speed delivery. Offer applies in U.K. only and is not valid to present subscribers. Silhouette reserve the right to exercise discretion in granting membership. If price changes are necessary you will be notified. Offer expires December 1985.

EPS1

Silhouette Desire

Your chance to write back!

We'll send you details of an exciting free offer from *SILHOUETTE*, if you can help us by answering the few simple questions below.

Just fill in this questionnaire, tear it out and put it in an envelope and post today to: Silhouette Reader Survey, FREEPOST, P.O. Box 236, Croydon, Surrey CR9 9EL. You don't even need a stamp.

What is the title of the *SILHOUETTE Desire* you have just read?

_____

How much did you enjoy it?

Very much ☐   Quite a lot ☐   Not very much ☐

Would you buy another *SILHOUETTE Desire* book?

Yes ☐   Possibly ☐   No ☐

How did you discover *SILHOUETTE Desire* books?

Advertising ☐   A friend ☐   Seeing them on sale ☐

Elsewhere (please state) _____

How often do you read romantic fiction?

Frequently ☐   Occasionally ☐   Rarely ☐

Name (Mrs/Miss) _____

Address _____

_____

_____ **Postcode** _____

Age group: Under 24 ☐   25–34 ☐   35–44 ☐

45–55 ☐   Over 55 ☐

Silhouette Reader Service, P.O. Box 236, Croydon, Surrey CR9 9EL.
Readers in South Africa—write to:
Silhouette Romance Club,
Private Bag X3010, Randburg 2125.

SD1